SALT & SEEDS

ALAN RAW

Grokkist

GROKKIST PRESS, AN IMPRINT OF GROKKIST LTD

This is the first edition of Salt & Seeds, published in 2025

paperback:- ISBN 978-1-0670803-1-0

hardback:- ISBN 978-1-0670803-2-7

ebook:- ISBN 978-1-0670803-0-3

Published by Grokkist Press, an imprint of Grokkist Ltd. Auckland New Zealand. A catalogue record for this book is available from the National Library of New Zealand.

For more information visit: grokk.ist/books/salt-and-seeds

Acknowledgements

I would like to thank Danu Poyner and the Grokkist
Network, the Schumacher Institute,
ASP (Association of Sustainability Practitioners),
The Creative & Cultural Organisation, The RSA, Writers@,
Pan Galactic, Sir Alec Gill, Rachel Lund, Theresa Samsome,
and all my other dear friends and family – especially my
sister Julie Margaret Alice,
brother Jim, uncle Vince Raw, my son Harrison Raw,
and my ever-tolerant wife Sara. x
Your support and inspiration has empowered me to
challenge the limits of my neurodiversity and start writing
again. I admire your patience and appreciate you all.

Alan

CONTENTS

Publisher's Preface   VII

Prologue   IX

1. Signs and Signals   1

2. Wild Knowledge   11

3. Ground Truth   21

4. Storm and Shelter   31

5. Constellation   41

6. Leviathan   51

7. Cassiopeia Rising   75

8. Connect and Thrive   89

9. Growth Rings   117

10. Seeds of Change   135

Glossary   163

About the Author   167

About You   169

PUBLISHER'S PREFACE

*S**alt & Seeds* is the first book published under the Grokkist Press imprint, and it feels entirely fitting that it should be this one.

Grokkist Press exists to nurture works that re-enchant our attention, rekindle ethical imagination, and offer practical hope for living and flourishing in an unfinished world.

We are drawn to creations that nourish rather than alarm – works that treat care as a form of courage, that resist the easy lure of cynicism, and that insist not on grand declarations, but on the slow, stubborn practice of flourishing.

Alan Raw's *Salt & Seeds* is a gift of precisely this kind. It is a story born of embodied wisdom, lived curiosity, and a radical trust in community—qualities that feel increasingly precious in a world that often mistakes acceleration for progress. It offers a vision of future-building not through grand revolutions, but through the quiet revolution of tending, connecting, and refusing to look away.

At Grokkist, we believe that imagination is a serious form of action, and that publishing is itself a generative practice—one that opens space for possibility to take root and grow.

Publishing this work is an act of faith in the unseen gardens it might inspire—on the page, in the soil, and in the slow work of becoming who we need to be.

We are honoured to share it with you.

Grokkist Press

PROLOGUE

The ice crumbled faster than anyone predicted, faster than the most alarmist models had dared suggest. The frosts of the northern lands vanished like morning dew under a hot sun. Warmer seas birthed greater storms with frightening frequency, each year bringing higher waters than the last. But it was the compound surge of 2059 that changed everything. That was when the North Sea truly began redrawing England's eastern edge, not with gentle brushstrokes, but with the violent hand of a frustrated artist. Three massive storms hit during spring tides, their timing as cruel as their strength. The first overwhelmed coastal defences, then, before recovery efforts were complete, two more arrived in quick succession. The third as days of rain drained from the hills, swelling rivers with nowhere to flow but into already flooded communities.

Now, after decades of displacement, and resilience, much has changed. Here lay the seeds of knowledge, taking root in transformed landscapes, sprouting unexpected truths about adaptation and survival.

Chapter 1

SIGNS AND SIGNALS

Whitby North Yorkshire

T he North Sea was gnawing at Yorkshire's crumbling cliffs, when Rowan Cullen noticed something unlikely in his satellite data.

After a year of monitoring coastal vegetation from the old signal station, he knew it would be a lot easier for him if the numbers added up. But there it was – chlorophyll signatures where nothing should grow. Plants thriving in soil that regular floods of salt water had rendered lifeless since the last surge. Not just surviving, but spreading, according to three consecutive imaging passes.

His Meridian hummed against his wrist, that particular caller's pulse pattern he'd learned to dread. With a reluctant gesture, he expanded the display, and Regina's face materialised before him, his supervisor at the Coastal Monitoring Consortium looming from the air like an unwelcome apparition.

"Your daily metrics are late again, Rowan!" Her face filled the view, perfect as always, not a silver rooted hair out of place, despite the early hour. Regina believed in procedure, it was how she'd risen from Field Researcher to Consortium Director in record time. "The board expects consistency in our reporting."

"The consistency is the problem," Rowan replied, running a hand through his perpetually uncombed hair. "The readings are strange. I'm seeing vegetation where nothing's grown for years."

"Whatever you're thinking," Regina cut in, "just stop it and file your report. Now, please, Rowan!" She hung up before he could protest. Then she sat forward, rubbing the side of her neck below her left ear, where tension seemed to build up and caused her pain, the board meeting that morning had been brutal. Thirty years of dedicated environmental science, reduced to quarterly metrics and impact assessments, that barely scratched the surface of what was actually happening.

"Anomalous readings," she muttered, staring at Rowan's preliminary data. Part of her – the scientist she'd been before climbing the administrative ladder – wanted to pursue this. But if she allocated resources to every enthusiastic observation from the field stations, they'd lose what little funding remained for the long-term monitoring programs.

She glanced at the proposal on her screen: a corporate partnership that promised stable financing for five more years. The kind of security that kept researchers employed, that maintained the databases tracking fifty years of coastal change. The document was littered with sustainability buzzwords, but beneath the greenwashing there was enough genuine science to make a difference. Not the difference she'd dreamed of making as a young researcher, perhaps, but tangible nonetheless.

"Sometimes all that matters is the lights staying on," she told herself – the mantra of career administrators everywhere. She swiped to send the standard metrics request to

Rowan again. Better he be disappointed, than have forty researchers lose their positions when the next funding review came around.

Through the curved windows of Rowan's station, the early sun caught the living solar arrays, crowning what remained of old Whitby. The coastline had transformed since the Antarctic collapse and subsequent sea rise. Great tidal surges had battered against their defences until the last great surge drowned the lower town completely.

Where there had once been seaside arcades and fish and chip shops, now floating gardens and pontoons threaded between the tops of drowned buildings, their foundations long since adapted into artificial reefs. The once-picturesque tourist town had evolved into a patchwork of elevated walkways, houseboats, and sustainable trade barges, their hulls grown rather than built in the marine-culture yards.

The old Abbey Steps rose from the new tideline to the small church and ancient abbey ruins – silent witnesses to centuries of change, now watching over yet another transformation.

Beyond the inhabited zone lay sector 7, where the sea-swept forest park had been abandoned to the elements, after repeated salination had made it "economically unfeasible" for regeneration, according to the consortium's bland reports.

Movement caught his eye and Rowan grabbed his binoculars, focusing on twisted trees at the sector's edge. A flash of vibrant green, and the way the small branches swayed... it didn't match the dead wood he was used to seeing. There was new movement in the morning breeze, leaves catching light in a way that dead branches never could.

His Meridian pulsed again at his wrist: another automated request for standardised metrics from the Coastal Monitoring Consortium. Rowan swiped the notification away. There was nothing standard about what he was seeing. With a fluid motion, he expanded the device's display, transforming it into a translucent screen that overlaid enhanced visuals, onto the windows and landscape beyond. The thermal bands showed definite biological activity. Even the reliable old radar backscatter was revealing patterns of new growth in the forest structure. He collapsed the Meridian back to wrist size, the living photosynthetic elements along its edge glowing softly as they charged in the morning sun.

The metrics could wait. This was exactly what he'd been searching for since he'd started at the station – something that didn't fit the models, something alive that shouldn't be. Something that might actually matter.

He was halfway down the signal station's spiral staircase when he heard voices below, unusual for this hour. Most of Whitby wouldn't stir for a while yet. What remained of the fishing fleet was already out and the market traders were still setting up. The voices echoed in the stone chamber – one he recognised as Isaac the Harbour Master, the other unfamiliar, carrying a lilt that didn't belong to Yorkshire.

"I hope the station officer is awake," a woman's voice, her accent distinctly Dutch, precise but musical.

"He's usually an early riser," Isaac replied in his deep salt-worn tone.

"I'll only need a few min – "

Rowan rounded the final curve and nearly collided with her. She wore practical seafaring clothes, a weather-beaten jacket of some self-repairing material, sturdy deck-boots that had clearly seen real work, and she carried a distinctive hexagonal sampling case, marked with the North Sea Seed Trust's emblem. The Trust was known for its work preserving coastal plant genetics, and rarely visited this little harbour.

"Dr Cullen?" she asked, steadying herself. Her eyes were a shade of blue he'd rarely seen before, a detail Rowan immediately noticed and then felt foolish for doing so.

"Just Rowan," he corrected, suddenly self-conscious of his rumpled appearance. "The doctorate's a bit... unfinished. I got this placement and they've kept me on." He was aware he had shared more information than expected, and felt he'd better move the conversation on.

"I'll leave you to get acquainted," Isaac said with an amused smile, as he turned back towards the harbour.

Isaac was tall, with strongly sculpted features, his skin wind-etched and rain-polished, like sea-worn rock. He had dark, watchful eyes that had seen more than he would ever tell, and his kind expression was framed by a knitted hat pulled low and a short, salt-white beard.

"Go steady now," he called as he left.

"You're here about sector seven, aren't you?" Rowan asked, looking back at his visitor.

Her eyebrows rose slightly, clearly surprised by the directness emerging from his initial waffle.

"Yes, I'm Ash Van der Meer." She extended her hand.

Rowan shook it and noticed her grip was firm.

"We've been tracking unusual patterns in the coastal vegetation. Your monitoring station has the best records for this stretch of coast, Rowan."

Her gaze travelled past him to the staircase leading up to his instruments, then she stepped around him and went up. There was something refreshingly straightforward about her, Rowan thought – no corporate veneer, just focused curiosity.

"The chlorophyll readings shouldn't be possible," Rowan said, turning to the wall map where he'd marked anomalous readings over the past weeks. "Nothing but the hardiest marsh grass can survive that level of long-term salt contamination."

"Not impossible," she replied thoughtfully, studying his markings. "Just unexpected. The question is whether your satellite data matches what's happening on the ground."

He held out his field kit that had been on his shoulder. "I was just heading out to check."

"Mind if I join you?" A small smile appeared at the corner of her mouth, as if she already knew his answer.

The morning sun transformed the North Sea from grey to silver, its surface rippled with wind patterns, but no great waves. Somewhere out there, in the sea-scoured ruins of the old coast, something was changing. Something that didn't follow the rules.

"I know a shortcut through the old sea defences," Rowan said, slinging his pack back over his shoulder. "But we'll need to move quickly, the weather's due to turn by mid-afternoon."

The old sea wall stood as a monument to failed engineering, its concrete face pitted and crumbling, rebar exposed like the bones of a beached whale. Wave-smoothed rubble made treacherous footing as they picked their way along its base. Yet ahead of them, impossibly, life bloomed – young elder and hawthorn pushing through broken concrete, young buckthorn where there had only been a ghost forest of dead wood.

"Look at this," Ash said, crouching to examine the vegetation. She pulled a sampling tool from her case, a sleek device that looked more like an artist's stylus than scientific equipment. "The leaf structures are unlike anything I've seen in these species."

Rowan knelt beside her, close enough to catch the faint scent of something herbal in her hair. The plants looked different – leaves thicker, with patterns of fine hairs and waxy coating, that seemed almost engineered for salt resistance. Rowan's soil testing kit showed unexpected readings: "The substrate chemistry is completely different from when they abandoned the area. These plants aren't just surviving here, they appear to be transforming their environment."

Ash carefully bagged a leaf sample, her movements precise. "They shouldn't be this close to the sea, let alone thriving. Unless..." She pulled what looked like an old botanical guide from her case, its cover worn but cherished. "There was research before the surges, about coastal plant communities developing salt tolerance, but nothing like this level of adaptation. I think this is quite unusual."

The microscope lens on her device revealed complex fungal networks around the roots. Patterns of unexpected interaction.

"It's as if they're collaborating," Rowan murmured, forgetting the metrics waiting in his To-do list, forgetting Regina's disapproval, forgetting everything but the extraordinary life beneath his fingertips. "Adapting together rather than competing."

Ash's eyes met his, reflecting the same wonder he felt. "Exactly what I've been looking for," she said.

CHAPTER 2

WILD KNOWLEDGE

A movement further down the track caught Rowan's eye – someone working among raised beds built behind the sea wall's shelter. He hadn't noticed the garden until now, tucked away in what had been a wind-torn wasteland.

"Someone's growing food here?" Ash asked, incredulously, shading her eyes against the strengthening sun.

"Oh, that will be Mae," Rowan replied, recognition dawning. "She lives up on the hill there and grows a lot of food for the community. Everyone thought she was mad to stay after the evacuation orders."

"Looks like there was method in her madness," Ash observed, as she picked up her kit.

The garden revealed itself as they drew closer, not the chaotic plot of a stubborn eccentric, but a complex arrangement of beds, built up in careful layers. Each section hosted different combinations of plants, some familiar, others were a rare sight even to Ash. Terracotta water catchments fed precise irrigation channels, and what looked like homemade sensors protruded from key points in the soil.

Mae straightened up as they approached, brushing earth from hands covered in tattoos, that extended up past muscular forearms. They weren't mere decoration, but a botanical record – beautifully inked into her skin. Grey-streaked hair protruded from a thick reddish brown woolly hat, that matched her jumper. Sharp, but kind eyes assessed them with a gardener's attention to detail.

"Wondered when someone would notice," she said, her Yorkshire accent warm with amusement. No introduction, no surprise at their presence, as if she'd expected them all along. "Been watching those trees for months now. Different, aren't they? Things are changing."

"You've been monitoring the changes?" Ash asked, professional interest evident in her tone.

"In my own way." Mae gestured at her little plot of land. "Feed the same soil for thirty years, you learn its rhythms. Like how these beans grew stronger once I let the local plants establish around them. Or how the soil structure changes where different root systems meet."

She crouched to pull aside some ground cover, revealing a complex interaction of roots below. "Nature's got her own ideas about balance. I do my best to read her messages." She looked up, eyes crinkling with the wisdom that comes from many years of patient observation. "Right now, they're saying, things are getting better."

Rowan watched Ash's expression shift from professional interest to genuine respect. The North Sea Seed Trust dealt with cutting-edge genetics and conservation science, yet here was Ash kneeling in mud beside a local gardener, treating her knowledge with the same deference she might show a senior researcher.

"These companion plantings," Ash said, pointing to a particularly lush section, "did you develop them through trial and error, or was there a pattern you recognised?"

"Bit of both," Mae replied, pleased at the question. "Started with what my mother taught me about permaculture. But the land kept changing, so the guilds had to change too. The plants will tell you what they need if you watch long enough. And I'm not the only one around here growing, we learn from each other, it's a good community."

"What are these?" Ash asked, crouching beside one of the unusual sensor devices, nestled among what looked like heritage tomato plants. Each appeared handcrafted – resin-sealed casings, housing complex sensor arrays. Some with tiny solar collectors that shifted like sunflowers to track the light.

"My little helpers," Mae replied, handing Ash a small trowel as if it were the most natural thing to share. "They watch what I can't."

Ash studied one more closely. "These aren't commercial."

"No, repurposed components mostly," Mae said, adjusting something beneath the soil. "The agricultural sensors available commercially take a reductionist approach – tracking basic nutrients and moisture. But gardens are complex adaptive systems. You need to understand the relationships between organisms, to truly support them."

"Like communities," Ash mused.

Mae smiled. "Exactly like that."

"Did you make them?"

"Just a hobby project," she said, changing the subject.

"I must crack on, but please stay and take samples if you like."

The afternoon past quickly as they documented and sampled. Rowan found himself creating new categories in his field notes – the changes they were seeing didn't fit any standard classification. Beyond the soil chemistry and plant adaptations, subtle shifts rippled through the whole ecosystem. Different insects moved among the new growth, a bird he hadn't seen in years gathered seeds from the maturing plants, and patterns of moisture retention defied the drought-flood cycles that had become the new normal. None of it seemed random or mere chance mutation.

The wind grew stronger, bringing the chill of an approaching storm. Mae looked up at the darkening sky, then down at their scattered sampling equipment.

"Best get inside before this lot gets soaked," she said, gathering her tools with efficiency. "Besides, I've got thirty years of records up at the cottage. Might be useful if you're interested in the whole story."

"We shouldn't impose..." Rowan began, but Ash was already helping Mae gather their equipment and silenced

Rowan with a look that clearly said this was too valuable an opportunity to miss, and she was not amused by his decision to speak for both of them.

"Knowledge wants to be shared," Mae said simply, leading them up a steep narrow track between salt-hardy herbs. Their fragrance, released by the first drops of rain, rose around them like an ancient welcome. "And you've been hiding in your tower since you got here, Rowan. You need to get to know us all a bit better," Mae insisted.

Her cottage seemed to grow from the landscape rather than being imposed upon it. Thick stone walls softened by climbing plants, windows positioned to catch light and warmth throughout the day. Solar panels and a small mariner's wind turbine crowned a grass-covered roof, which was home to a few cheeky dandelions that Mae clearly welcomed. Rain gutters fed water butts; a grey-water pipe irrigated a terraced reed bed beside the stone steps. Everything connected, everything serving multiple purposes. Behind the cottage they could see rich green planting in concentric circles – no soil visible, just plants of every height, supported by hazel sticks, all growing together. A little food forest, full of life.

Inside, the little cottage welcomed them with the same integrated efficiency. Preserved foods lined walls of shelves, made from reclaimed timber. Mae moved around the space with gentle ease, setting an old kettle to boil, on an antique electric cooker, wired into a complex circuit of inverters and batteries. They were all fixed to her kitchen wall, below a thick slate worktop, covered with jars of spices and herbs.

"Teas? I've got wild mint and lemon balm from out back," she said, "Unless you'd prefer nettle? Good for circulation after a chill."

Ash had paused by Mae's bookshelf, noticing a small framed photo, partially hidden behind a jar of dried seaweed. It was Mae, younger but unmistakable, receiving some kind of award. She looked very smart.

"Nettle please," Ash replied and Rowan asked for the same, thinking Ash probably knew best.

As Mae passed the mug, Ash noticed the faded tattoo on her inner forearm - a crescent moon and helix design, with an old-style Greek harp beneath.

"Nice ink," Ash commented.

"Thank you, I like my flowers," Mae said smiling.

"That one looks like the Life Seed Project logo."

"Ah, yes I was a fan, a lifetime ago, and took inspiration from the design," Mae replied with a slight smile.

"Me too! I was only little when it launched, though."

Before they could take a sip, the door burst open. An excited teenager rushed in, clutching a notebook with pages fluttering.

"Mae, the samphire's growing in a new pattern near the old wreck, and I think..."

They stopped short, rain-damp curls clinging to their forehead, brown eyes wide with surprise at the unexpected guests. Alert and wary, the young arrival hovered in the doorway, sketchbook still clutched tight in one hand – analysing Ash and Rowan in startled fascination.

"Perfect timing, Cass," Mae said with a fond glance at the newcomer. "Meet our signal station watcher and our special guest from the Seed Trust. Seems they've noticed what you've been drawing."

Cassiopeia's initial shyness dissolved into enthusiasm that seemed too large for their slight frame.

"The patterns? Look!" They turned their notebook to reveal careful sketches of vegetation spread, leaf shapes, insects, and soil changes, each precisely dated and located. Not the casual observations of a hobbyist, but the systematic documentation of a natural scientist in the making.

Rowan looked impressed, running a finger along a particularly detailed sketch of root systems.

"These are wonderful. You've captured exactly what we were seeing today."

Cass's eyes widened, clearly unused to having their work validated by someone with official credentials.

"Most people think I'm just being weird, drawing plants," they said, a slight defensive edge in their voice that spoke of past dismissals.

"The best scientists," Ash said, accepting a steaming mug from Mae, "are the ones who pay attention to details others miss. These are more than just detailed – they're methodical. You've been tracking changes over time, correlating different factors..." She paused, studying a particularly complex diagram. "This is exactly the kind of baseline data we need."

The tension in Cass's thin shoulders eased slightly.

"Really? You actually want to know about this stuff?"

"More than want," Rowan said, surprised by the certainty in his own voice. "We need to understand what's happening here, and this helps."

Ash glanced at Mae, who was arranging berries and homemade biscuits on a wooden tray.

"Would you be willing to share your records? Both the historical data and these new observations?"

"That's what they're for," Mae said, gesturing at walls covered in maps and charts, each marked with different handwriting, some faded with age, others fresh and bold. "Fisher-folk note the wildlife changes. Old folks remember what grew where, before. Even the kids help, they've got sharp eyes, once you teach them what to look for in rock pools."

Rowan moved closer to examine a detailed chart tracking soil salinity changes over decades. The data points were methodical, the observations meticulous. Official science would dismiss it as amateur work, yet he couldn't deny the rigour behind it. This wasn't just gardening; it was a multi-generational research project, conducted without grants or institutional backing.

Through the window, the lights of the bay began to flicker on as evening gathered and rain tapped against the glass.

Somewhere out there, life was finding new ways to thrive in poisoned ground. The question on Rowan's mind was: would human institutions be flexible enough to recognise and learn from what was happening?

Delighted by the interest in their work, Cass sat down and began adding the day's observations to their notebook, face intent with concentration. While Mae kept Ash and Rowan busy by digging out more records to share. Cass considered the impact of Ash's arrival. Tomorrow would bring more changes to log, more patterns to understand. 'Proper' scientists might not consider their notebook data valid, they thought, but nature doesn't care about all that. If they just kept watching, recording, and showing anyone willing to look, eventually someone should take their work seriously. Cass looked up at Ash, who was examining Mae's work with genuine interest, and Cass began to feel something they hadn't felt before: an excitement, born of hope that this unusual woman may be the mentor they'd been longing for.

CHAPTER 3

GROUND TRUTH

T he consortium's response arrived at dawn, his Meridian warming subtly against his skin before projecting the message into his field of vision: "URGENT: Unauthorised research protocols detected. All monitoring to be for authorised searches only, effective immediately. Report to virtual meeting room at 09:00."

The message pulsed with corporate red in the air before him, a stark contrast to the soft morning light filtering through the signal station's eastern windows. Rowan passed his hand through the projection, watching it ripple around his fingers as the Meridian's sensors tracked his movement.

Below the message, satellite data confirmed what Mae had told him, three new growth sites emerging along the coast. The evidence was mounting, too much to ignore. As Mae had said, things were definitely changing.

Through his window, Rowan could see Cass teaching a small group of younger children how to use Mae's soil testing methods in the community garden. Their movements were deliberate, their focus absolute. They'd documented more changes in a week than his official reports had captured in months.

His Meridian chimed sharply, then expanded without his input, the consortium's executive protocols overriding his privacy settings. The composite stretched from wrist to palm, forming a temporary screen where Regina's face appeared, her usual professional mask showing cracks of strain around the eyes. The device's environmental sensors registered his spike in heart rate, adjusting the display's brightness to soften the intrusion.

"Your initial findings are... concerning," she began carefully, "The consortium requires consistency across all monitoring stations. You have no idea what a headache this is causing with the board.

"The funding implications alone..." She glanced away for a moment, a flicker of something beyond institutional concern crossing her face. "Our corporate partners have expectations about commercially viable research. Aadan Zhao at Noah Ecosystems in particular, has been pressuring the board about potential applications." She collected herself visibly. "I've engaged Enviroconnex. They'll be heading your way to conduct a proper professional assessment. Please make sure they have everything they need."

"But we've already got a monitoring network developing here," Rowan protested, gesturing toward his window where the community's research continued below. "People who've watched this coast change for decades. They have data going back to before the surge that..."

"Citizen science has its place," Regina cut in, her tone dismissive yet strained. "But we need peer-reviewed methodologies. Proper risk assessments. The consortium can't be liable for unauthorised field researchers, trampling through sensitive areas."

"Mae's garden is hardly 'trampling'..."

"Rowan." Regina's voice hardened. "Your position at the station is already precarious. Don't make this difficult. Dr Ghadah from Enviroconnex will arrive tomorrow with her team. Give them whatever they need, and perhaps we can salvage something from this... irregularity." The screen went dark before he could respond.

Rowan sat motionless, staring into space. Two years of dutiful monitoring, of sending reports that disappeared into the consortium's databases. They were never questioned because they confirmed what everyone already believed – that the coast was dead, beyond recovery, a sacrifice zone to be studied but not saved.

Until now.

He grabbed his jacket and headed downstairs, uncertainty knotting his stomach. The tide was low, exposing stretches of what had once been seafront promenade, now transformed into a complex intertidal zone. He traced the path to where Ash had moored her research vessel, The Wild Margin.

He'd been getting to know the sleek boat since Ash's arrival, and it had now become an unofficial gathering point for local observers. Its innovative design – solar skin, hydrofoils that allowed it to skim above rather than through sensitive ecosystems, and sails that captured both wind and solar energy – represented everything the consortium's rigid, institutional approach couldn't capture.

"Enviroconnex are coming," he announced without preamble as he stepped aboard.

Ash looked up from her microscope, a strand of copper hair escaping her practical braid.

"Let me guess – comprehensive feasibility study? Environmental impact assessment?"

"Six months just to design the research protocols." He slumped onto a lab stool, running a hand through his knotted hair.

"They want everything done their way, through proper channels."

"While nature carries on regardless," Ash said, adjusting her scope. "Look at these root structures – the mycorrhizal networks are connecting species that have never been documented growing together before."

The vessel's cabin door opened. Mae entered with Cass and a stocky, long-haired dog with the unmistakable black and white markings of a border collie but with a tan patch across one eye. He trotted then waited, looking back as the boat dipped with the weight of a large arrival. Cassiopeia's grandfather, Old Isaac, stepped in. He was the Harbour Master and his weather-beaten face held a lifetime of maritime knowledge, his calloused hands carefully unfolding a hand-drawn chart across the lab bench.

The dog, circled the space before returning to Isaac's side, desperate to meet everyone on board.

"Sidown Bram," Isaac murmured absently, the dog immediately obeying while keeping watchful eyes on everyone in the room. One bottom fang poked out at an odd angle from his mouth, giving him a permanently sceptical expression.

"Found something you need to see," Isaac said, pointing to patches marked in careful detail. "Sea plants growing where industrial run-off cleared them long ago. Nothing's grown there since I was younger than Cass. Different now though."

"Grandad's taking me out to the locations," Cass added, notebook ready, eyes bright with anticipation. "I can't wait to see what's living in there. Crabs, I hope, I love crustaceans. Do you think it's connected to what we're seeing on shore?"

Rowan thought about translating all this local data into Enviroconnex's standardised formats. The careful observations of people who knew every tide and current reduced to data points in a glacially slow preliminary survey. Reports that would be filed away in digital archives, reviewed by people who'd never felt this soil beneath their fingertips or watched these waters change through decades of pollution and storms.

"Some scientists are coming and they'll want to start from scratch," he said, unable to keep the frustration from his voice. "Their sampling protocols, their testing methods. All this..." he gestured at their accumulated knowledge, the charts and notebooks, "won't count."

He saw Cass's young face fall, enthusiasm draining away. "Sorry, Cass. I value what you're doing – I'm just trying to manage expectations. I know what this lot are like."

An uncomfortable silence fell. Mae's expression remained neutral, but her shoulders tensed slightly. Isaac looked down at his charts, annoyed but not surprised, that a lifetime of knowledge could be deemed irrelevant by institutional authority.

"Then maybe it's time to try something different," Ash said, breaking the silence. She turned to the group, a new intensity in her gaze. Bramley jumped up to listen "How many boats in the local fleet?"

"Seven still working," Isaac replied, puzzled. "Why?"

"And how many others like Cass, keeping records?"

Mae smiled, catching on. "Dozens, up and down the coast. More if you count those who remember how things used to be."

"The consortium wants proper scientific monitoring?" Ash's eyes gleamed with something that made Rowan's pulse quicken. "Let's give them something they can't ignore. Not scattered observations, but a coordinated network. Systematic sampling, regular monitoring..."

"We'd need to standardise the recording methods," Rowan said, warming to the idea despite himself.

"But our methods," Cass interrupted. "Ones that capture what we're seeing, not just what fits what they want."

Isaac nodded slowly, considering. "We'd need a way to share findings. The fishing fleet's scattered, but we all come back to harbour."

"I could set up a data hub," Cass offered, their confidence growing. "Mae taught me how, I'll make it simple to work with everyone's devices, even Grandad's ancient tablet."

Mae had been silent, but now she spoke. "Knowledge has always grown this way," she said. "From the ground up. Before there were universities, there was just people sharing. No reason it can't work now, especially with all the equipment you have."

"Mae knows systems." said Isaac "Her research will stand up to anyone's scrutiny."

"Alright Isaac," Mae said, with an air of embarrassment as she threw Bram a biscuit from her pocket, which he saw coming and caught effortlessly. When Isaac raised his eyebrow, she shrugged unapologetically.

"He'll be too fat to get up the stairs if you keep that up," Isaac grumbled, but there was no real annoyance in his voice.

Through the lab window, they could see Dr Ghadah and the Enviroconnex team, arriving a day earlier than expected, crisp in their corporate outfits, their autonomous transport already taking off again behind them. Her team followed her, wheeling cases of equipment up the harbour walk. Soon there would be meetings, consultations, matrices and methodologies. All the ingredients for a funding application that would take months to process.

But out there in soil and water, life was writing its own protocols. Perhaps it was time for official science to adapt to reality, rather than trying to force reality into predetermined boxes.

"I'm heading South," Ash said quietly, her focus on adjusting a sample under her microscope. "Following the adaptation patterns down the coast. I could use someone who knows how to read the signals from above." She glanced up, meeting Rowan's eyes. "And you could use a change of perspective. How are your sea legs?"

"Rusty," Rowan replied with a laugh that didn't quite hide his uncertainty. "I'll think about it."

In reality, his mind was already racing ahead of his caution. The consortium's satellites would show these changes spreading along the coastline, whether their analysts acknowledged them or not. Someone needed to ground-truth the data, to connect the aerial view with what was happening at soil level. He looked at his Meridian, the device quietly collecting environmental data even as it rested against his wrist. He knew he could access satellite feeds from anywhere – the European Space Agency's data remained open-source even as corporate information became increasingly proprietary. He could connect his Meridian to his own quantum-secured storage. Set up his own firewall to stop the consortium switching it off if necessary.

He felt uneasy as unfamiliar thoughts took root. These were dangerous ideas, career-ending ideas. The tower was his home and the consortium owned it. They also paid his wages – modest but enough to live on in a world where economic stability had become as unpredictable as the weather. But something had shifted inside him since meeting the harbour's new seafarer.

He looked at her, already deep in conversation with Cass about sampling methodologies, the natural authority with which she empowered rather than directed the community, was impressive. The feeling that had been growing since their first meeting finally revealed its meaning: She represented everything he'd once believed science could be – collaborative, adaptive, alive.

That evening, he stood at his computer, staring at the resignation letter on his screen. The tower had been his refuge since the last surge – stable, secure, above the chaos below. But now... he looked at The Wild Margin in the harbour, its solar skin rippling in the sunset like living tissue. The Wild Margin versus his comfortable tower. Movement versus stasis. Growth versus certainty.

He wasn't sure he could take the risk.

The following morning, something had cleared, like sediment settling after a storm. He watched Cass and the other researchers below; their movements deliberate despite everything. Then he saw Enviroconnex workers heading down to erect cordons around Mae's garden, preparing to secure the site for assessment. The corporate method suddenly felt alien – clinical terms applied to living things.

In that moment, Rowan understood what truly separated his old life from what beckoned ahead: one observed from safe distance while the other demanded presence, participation, risk. His finger hovered over his Meridian for three heartbeats before he pressed send on two messages: his resignation to the consortium and his acceptance to Ash's invitation.

His hands trembled slightly – not from fear but from a strange, unexpected lightness. Is this what freedom feels like, he thought, terrifying but exactly right.

He began to pack what little he needed.

CHAPTER 4

STORM AND SHELTER

T he Wild Margin proved more than a boat, it was a testament to how technology could work with nature. Fifty feet of innovative design, the wide beam housing both living space and a compact laboratory, that doubled as its command centre.

"Dr Dahl's finest work," Ash explained as she guided Rowan through the vessel's systems, on their second day at sea. "Caused quite a stir when I first sailed from the Netherlands. The Dutch Maritime Authority couldn't decide whether to classify this as experimental technology or conventional vessel."

Self-optimising photovoltaic skin rippled like kelp in the morning light, while twin hydrofoils lifted the sleek hull above the waves at Ash's command, minimising impact on the delicate ecosystem below. In the shallows, they could retract the keel, exploring where other research vessels wouldn't dare venture. The sails and solar-electric drive, moved them silently through sensitive habitats, leaving nothing but displaced water in their wake.

The compact lab space had initially seemed chaotic to Rowan, but he quickly recognised the careful organisation behind Ash's apparent disorder. She had integrated his monitoring equipment with her analysis systems, creating something more effective than either could manage alone. His satellite data now fed directly into her coastal mapping program, while her field samples provided ground truth for his remote sensing.

"Pass me that calibration weight," Ash said, her focus on realigning a sensitive instrument that the morning's rough seas had disturbed.

Rowan handed her the precisely machined metal disc, watching her deft movements with undisguised admiration. There was something compelling about someone so completely at home in this changing world. While he had spent a year hiding in his tower, analysing data at a distance, Ash moved through the physical reality of their changing planet with confident grace.

"Have you lived on board long?" he asked, still adjusting to the gentle roll of the deck beneath his feet.

"Three years," she replied, not looking up from her task. "Before that, I was land-based at the Trust's research station." She glanced up, "But you can't understand coastal ecosystems without being part of them."

They'd ventured further out than planned, following traces of adaptation into deeper waters.

The ruins of old gas platforms rose from the sea like ancient monoliths to mankind's hubris, their bases now hosting complex ecosystems. Rowan could see fish darting among artificial reef structures that had grown spontaneously around the corroding supports.

"Whoa!" Rowan gasped, stumbling backwards, as the sea breached with a blast of air shooting up on their starboard side. A massive dark form had surfaced, water cascading from its barnacled skin.

"It's huge!" he cried, heart pounding against his ribs. "Fifty feet at least. I've never been this close."

"She's a Humpback," Ash replied, her voice steady as she made an entry in her observation log, though her eyes betrayed the same excitement Rowan felt.

Smoothly the mighty whale resubmerged, and through the hull's transparent sections, they watched it slowly cross beneath them, turning to see them as it passed. Its ancient eye seeming to study their presence with quiet intelligence.

"They're following the changing movements of their food" Ash explained. "Not many left like her now." The whale's fluke disappeared into the dark depths, leaving them alone in the vastness of the North Sea.

That's when they noticed the first signs of the storm.

The sky to the Northeast had turned the colour of bruised metal, a darkness gathering on the horizon that hadn't been there minutes before. They had been so engrossed in their work that they'd missed the sensor warning on the monitor, and now the barometer beeped its urgent alarm.

The Wild Margin's systems responded automatically, solar sails furling, hydrofoils appearing from the hull, adjusting their angle to maintain stability, but the wind arrived with unexpected force. Waves built faster than the computers could compensate for, the vessel's bow rising and falling with increasing violence.

"Hold on!" Ash called; her hands steady on the controls as another wind-swept wave crashed over the bow. The boat's biomimetic hull flexed and adapted, but even the most advanced technology had its limits against the raw power of the new storms that now ruled the North Sea.

Rowan lunged across the deck to secure their samples as the boat pitched violently. Hours of careful documentation could be lost in moments.

"Leave them!" shouted Ash as Rowan reached for a floating sample case with the boat hook. "We'll come back tomorrow!"

The next wave nearly took him overboard. Only Ash's quick grab at his life jacket saved him, pulling him into the relative safety of the helm, as the storm began to rage around them.

"Put your harness on and hold tight," she commanded, her voice carrying a certainty that left no room for argument.

Ash reached for her Helm helmet and put it on quickly, its AR visor connecting immediately and displaying sensor data from the Helm AI. This would maintain her awareness, despite the spray that now rendered conventional visibility impossible. It was designed for solo sailing in exactly these conditions. Through the smart glass, she could see the wave patterns, other vessels, and cardinal points that normal vision could no longer discern.

Knowing they couldn't outrun this storm, Ash made her decision. She dropped the sails completely and turned the bow directly into the waves, a motion that seemed counterintuitive to Rowan until he saw how it let them cut through each swell rather than being rolled sideways. The electric motors kicked in at full power, and they maintained position against the wind. They would weather the front, then work their way out to safety.

Ash maintained a calm exterior to reassure Rowan, but inside she felt the cold grip of responsibility. With no sailing experience and no protective gear of his own beyond a coat and life jacket, Rowan was completely dependent on her judgment. After years of solo sailing, the weight of another's safety felt foreign and terrifying.

Her eyes fixed on the Wild Margin's sensors in her visor display, not daring to blink as she searched for safe passage. The Helm AI followed her voice commands for different views while she held the wheel tightly. Checking the sonar and radar, desperate to avoid being smashed onto one of the barely submerged old industrial structures, or into another struggling ship, as they approached the coastline. Visibility through the windscreen was zero, awash with rain, while they faced the storm head-on.

She had to trust the technology as her guide until the worst had passed. This tech had gotten her through worse in the past, but the stakes were higher with Rowan's welfare in her hands. Some of the Wild Margin's equipment was a little old, as Ash had sourced it from repair stores on shore and mended it multiple times, but the Helm system was core to the Wild Margin's design and had never let her down.

Slowly but surely, they made their way out. They were much further North than intended, but could now track back close to the coast for a few hours, then find a mooring spot to spend the night.

Later, anchored in a sheltered cove, Rowan opened a bottle of Mae's homemade elderberry wine that had somehow survived the chaos. They had hardly spoken since the storm hit and a tension between them lingered, evident in the way they avoided looking directly at one another.

Rowan broke the silence first.

"For a moment there, I thought we weren't going to make it," Rowan admitted, handing Ash a wooden mug. The cabin, after the storm, felt surprisingly cosy as the Wild Margin's systems hummed a low, reassuring thrum.

"The sea was just reminding us who's in charge.... it does that a lot," Ash said, accepting the mug. Her usual assertiveness was softened, replaced by a thoughtful, quieter side that

Rowan hadn't seen before. "My father would have said it's the gods testing us."

"Are you religious?" Rowan asked, genuinely curious. It seemed an odd juxtaposition to her usual scientific approach.

She smiled, swirling the wine thoughtfully. "More of a Buddhist these days, I think." She took a sip and looked uncharacteristically vulnerable, like she was not accustomed to sharing her personal preferences. "I wouldn't blame nature for being angry at us, though. Is that religious?"

"No, I don't think so. It's the sort of thing my Irish Mum used to say. "She was into the old nature magic stuff, talking to trees and all that. My Dad thought she was mad."

"What did he believe in?" Ash asked shuffling closer like she was getting more interested in the conversation.

"He was Roman Catholic, but he lost his faith in the church, and everything, after the floods kept coming up the Humber." Rowan looked into his mug, then topped it up as forgotten memories began surfacing. "First, we couldn't get insurance on the house he built, then we couldn't sell it to move away. We were busy helping build walls and filling sandbags, while some were still saying there was nothing to worry about." He paused and glanced up at Ash's attentive face, Mae's potent elixir was beginning to warm him from the inside, loosening his usual reserve. "When the first really big storms hit, I think I was about sixteen, I was out of school already. We took in evacuees at first, but they just kept coming. Hull's defences were no match for the surges. We ended up being refugees like everyone else we knew. It's all under water now."

"Is that why you chose the signal tower? Its elevation?"

Rowan nodded, surprised by her perceptive question.

"Best perk of the job. A good distance above the waterline. That's not going to help me now though, is it!" He added more wryly. "I was safe till you turned up." He laughed.

Ash accepted the dig with good humour. "And what about you?" Ash enquired. "What do you believe in?"

"Dad said I was like Doubting Thomas in the Bible; I'd only believe in what I could see for myself. After today..." He glanced around at their scattered equipment. "I believe I'm very small and the sea is very big. Thanks for grabbing me."

"You're welcome." She said with a smile.

Something shifted between them in that moment – an acknowledgment of shared vulnerability, perhaps, or the strange intimacy that comes from facing danger together.

"Tomorrow we'll find a town with a market and chandlery," Ash said, breaking the moment with practical concerns. "You need a safety helmet, gloves, and comms. My throat still hurts from shouting at you." She laughed, "But I'm sure it won't be the last time. I need to teach you to sail."

Through the cabin's skylights, the familiar waxing gibbous moon was clearly visible, the storm clouds having moved inland. The Wild Margin rocked gently, its systems adapting to the settling sea.

"You know what Mae would say?" Rowan mused, feeling the wine's warmth spread through him. "Nature can't be angry at us, because we are part of nature."

"We are nature studying itself," Ash added, while she hooked a hammock across the lab for Rowan's bunk.

"That's pretty deep," said Rowan teasingly, though the idea resonated more than he cared to admit.

After a while, they ventured up on deck and Ash lit a citronella oil burner to deter the mosquitoes. Then they sat in comfortable silence under a shared thermal blanket. Ash pointed out a star that she could recognise above the satellites – mechanical eyes watching the earth, gathering data that would soon show the patterns they were tracing by hand.

"Do you know your way around the night sky?" Ash asked.

"I know a few stars but not enough to navigate by," Rowan admitted. "There was too much light pollution where I grew up."

"Look there," she pointed upward. "Cassiopeia. The W-shaped constellation. Reminds me of our young friend."

"Named for a queen who got in trouble with the gods," Rowan recalled.

"I think our Cass was named for the stars themselves, not the myth," Ash said hopefully. "The middle of the W points to the North Star, a sure guide in the darkness."

Tomorrow they'd return to their sampling site, document their observations, add more data points to their growing understanding. But for now, they had this moment of quiet reflection, born from storm and survival, shared between two people learning to see the world through new eyes.

Rowan glanced at Ash, her profile outlined in moonlight, looking up. She had saved his life today without hesitation. He wondered what else might be possible between them, out here where old rules and boundaries seemed to dissolve into the vast horizon.

CHAPTER 5

CONSTELLATION

"The plants aren't just surviving here – they're changing how they grow together," Cass's message read as they anchored near Boggle Hole. The accompanying photographs showed intricate root systems and fungal networks, alongside data from Mae's experimental plots. In two months, Cass's observations had evolved from simple sketches to sophisticated ecological analysis, that would put many graduate students to shame.

"Look at how these species are interacting," Rowan said, showing Ash the images on their shared display. "That's professional-level ecosystem analysis."

"Cass has been trading notes with a youth group in the Netherlands," Ash replied, adjusting The Wild Margin's power cells to capture the afternoon sun. "They're seeing similar patterns in the Wadden Sea."

Rowan swiped through more images – systematic documentation of plant communities, reshaping their environments.

"This is spreading faster than I realised."

"That's what happens when you connect observers who care," Ash said, a note of pride in her voice. "Citizen Science can provide so much data, that you can see change happening in near real-time. "Institutional science moves at the pace of funding cycles and shares results when publication schedules allow. These kids move fast, they're curious, there's a lot of them and they're sharing all the time."

What had started as casual data sharing between coastal communities was growing into something larger, something with its own momentum. Norwegian fishing families compared notes with French salt marsh gardeners. Danish coastal farmers exchanged soil samples with English citizen scientists. A web of knowledge, spreading as naturally as the plants they studied. Unconstrained by the artificial boundaries of institutions.

Later that week, after a day with the community in Robin Hood's Bay. They rowed out in the Wild Margin's tender, to where they had anchored earlier. As he worked the oars Rowan looked at the shore and realised how much his perspective had changed in just two months at sea. He saw the coastline now, not as a disaster zone to be studied, but as a living community of adaptation.

Mae had invited them to join a meeting streaming from her cottage. Cass was hosting their first international visual call with the group. Mae's weathered stone building had been temporarily transformed into a high-tech hub, with

Cass's salvaged equipment creating an improvised but functional command centre.

"You've been busy," Ash observed, joining the call early to wish Cass luck.

"Reconnected some old satellite dishes," Cass explained, their usual reticence gone when discussing technical matters. "Better bandwidth than the public mesh. Mae configured the distributed authentication protocols," Cass added proudly. "I couldn't get the security handshakes working, but Mae knew exactly how to modify the access permissions."

Mae looked up from adjusting a delicate component. "Just remembered some basics from another life," she said lightly. The casual dismissal didn't match the confident precision of her movements as she calibrated equipment that would have challenged most communications engineers.

Rowan and Ash watched as Cass confidently welcomed the network as they logged on. They facilitated the sharing of findings with the young citizen scientists joining from across Europe. The teenager's growth in just two months was remarkable – not just in knowledge but in the calm authority with which they presented complex findings.

"The sea lavender and cord grass aren't just growing side by side," Cass explained, showing microscope images so detailed that Rowan wondered where they'd gotten the equipment. "They're supporting each other. The grass stabilises the soil while the lavender's deep roots bring up nutrients. But look what happens where they meet..."

The plants had developed extensive fungal networks in the soil – textbook mutualism, but between species that shouldn't typically associate. The network participants were adapting not just individually but collectively, creating micro-environments that could withstand conditions none could survive alone.

"We're seeing similar patterns here," said Hendrik from the Netherlands, as he shared his evidence in the virtual space. He was a young man perhaps a year or two older than Cass. "The soil bacteria are different too – like they're evolving alongside the plants. Each community is slightly different, but they're all finding new ways to stabilise these changing environments."

"This is valuable research," Cass said, viewing the data with appreciation. "But the correlation coefficient isn't quite right. It should be 0.73, not 0.67."

Hendrik frowned, checking his work. After a moment, his eyebrows rose in surprise.

"You're right," he said, clearly impressed. "How did you spot that so quickly?"

"Numbers just... make patterns in my head," Cass replied with a small shrug, "Always have."

Mae, who was listening off camera, exchanged a meaningful glance with Isaac. There was pride in her eyes, but something more complex too – a guardian's quiet vigilance.

The excitement in the call was building, voices from France, Denmark, and Norway contributing observations that confirmed a pattern spreading across the North Sea basin. These weren't isolated anomalies but a coordinated response, as if life itself was networking just as these young observers were.

"We should share this with everyone," Cass suggested, their conviction growing visibly as ideas flowed. "Not just virtually – a real gathering. A festival of coastal science and adaptation."

The idea caught fire immediately, young observers offering suggestions and resources. Hendrik's mentor knew of funding available for such initiatives. Someone else had contacts with a wildlife charity – interested in supporting young researchers. Cass agreed to start the planning process, their hands already scribbling notes, and they set a date to meet again.

Rowan saw an expression on Cass's face he'd never observed before – not just excitement or intellectual curiosity, but something deeper. Purpose. Belonging. After everyone had said goodbye, Ash and Rowan stayed on to talk to Cass.

"That was impressive," Rowan said. "You've created something important here."

"It wasn't just me," Cass replied, though their eyes shone with deserved pride. "Everyone's contributing."

Later that evening, after the call, Ash sent a message to Dr Dahl. The Dutch designer rarely missed a chance to see his favourite creation in action, and he'd be eager to demonstrate the Wild Margin's innovative features at such a festival. He might even bring his own vessel, the Zonne-Zeevaarder – his latest prototype building on what they'd learned from the Wild Margin's years of service.

"He'll come," Ash said with certainty. "Dahl loves nothing more than seeing young people engage with bio-mimetic design."

Watching Cass present with such confidence, Rowan thought about how different this was from his own academic path – the rigid structures, the hierarchies, the slow, cautious accumulation of credibility and certifications, that only the privileged or sponsored could afford these days. Cass had bypassed all of that, creating knowledge through passion and collaborative sharing. The group's potential was inspiring... and slightly terrifying in its implications for institutions like the consortium. But was it adequate? There were reasons for the institutional processes, that had been developed over centuries, and the absence of them here was a little disconcerting.

"Regina's going to explode when she hears about this," he said, unable to suppress a smile at the thought.

"Good," Ash replied, her grin mischievous. "Maybe it'll shake up their thinking. They're not bad people, Rowan, just trapped in old structures that don't fit the world anymore."

"I hope you're right," he said nervously. "I hope we're not setting Cass up for a fall, or misleading her in any way, with unrealistic expectations."

"Is that what we're doing?" Ash asked, sounding a little defensive.

"Not intentionally," he said, sensing her disapproval.

"Not at all!" Ash stated firmly. The conversation was clearly closed, but Rowan couldn't shake his sense of unease.

Reports flowed in daily: unusual growth patterns around Northumberland pier footings, new species assemblages in Suffolk's contaminated soil, birds returning to Poole Harbour that hadn't been seen in decades. Each observation added another dimension to the emerging picture of coastal adaptation.

"It makes more sense when you look at it together," Rowan said one morning, comparing satellite data with the growing database of ground observations. "It's not just individual species adapting, it's entire communities working in concert."

"Like we are," Ash added with a smile that made Rowan's pulse quicken in a way that had nothing to do with scientific discovery.

"I've checked Cassiopeia's findings against the samples we collected at Robin Hood's Bay," Rowan said, beckoning Ash toward the microscope. "Take a look for yourself."

Ash leaned in, her shoulder brushing his as she adjusted the focus. Through the lens, she could see how the plants had developed root structures that showed remarkable adaptation to the changing environment. "I see them," Ash confirmed, "networks of fine tendrils interwoven with fungal threads, allowing different species to share resources and stabilise their surroundings. Clever little things."

"Like the old mycorrhizal networks in forests," Rowan said, "But this is at another level. These are species that evolved separately, now finding ways to support each other.

Through their regular calls with the cottage, they watched Cass's understanding deepen, their passion growing. Each conversation revealed not just new ecological observations but a young person growing into their own power, seeing how their individual efforts contributed to the larger picture.

"I've applied for the ecology programme," Cass announced, after the other participants had left one evening, face glowing with pride on the small screen. "They said my practical research experience was 'exceptional.' The scholarship interview is next week."

"That's brilliant!" Ash exclaimed. "They'd be fools not to take you."

Cass's expression grew more serious. "If I get in... I won't give up the network. Academic science needs what we're building here."

"That's exactly right," Rowan said, something lightening in his chest. Here was the future he'd once imagined for himself, before caution and security had driven him to the tower's isolation. Cass represented a different path – not abandoning formal science, but transforming it from within.

"I can't say I want you to go." Mae said with a look of worry and care. "I wish it was distance learning. You'll need a few lessons in independent living before you leave us."

"I'll be fine," Cass said confidently. "I can take care of myself."

"Our Shambhala Warrior," Ash said with a face filled with celebration.

Mae nodded and smiled, but Rowan could see the tension in her face and shoulders – motherly concern perhaps, or something more specific lurking beneath. She was clearly reticent.

That night, aboard The Wild Margin, Rowan updated their database, satellite data, chemical analyses and Cass's meticulous observations. The screen glowed with Hendrik's bacterial studies and fisherfolk's reports, each pixel a tiny beacon. Not just numbers and charts, but a constellation of human connections, people reading hope in the transformed coastline just as their ancestors once navigated by stars.

The network that had begun with Mae's garden was spreading, taking root in communities all along the coasts. And like the plants they studied, these connections were creating something more resilient than any could achieve alone.

As he worked, Rowan was conscious of Ash moving about the cabin, preparing their evening meal. The easy rhythm they'd developed over weeks at sea, felt as natural now as breathing, they just took turns to do what was needed, without much discussion. He thought about Cass's words – about the best scientists being those who know how to really look at things – and wondered what else he might see if he allowed himself to truly observe the connection growing between himself and Ash. What might be possible, if he let down the barriers he'd so carefully maintained?

The thought both terrified and exhilarated him, much like the storm they'd weathered together. Perhaps that was the lesson in all of this – that growth always involved risk, and venturing into uncharted waters. Perhaps, like the plants reclaiming poisoned ground, the reward was worth the danger.

CHAPTER 6

LEVIATHAN

Months had passed since Rowan left his life behind to sail away with Ash. The time had flown by as their coastal survey became an exciting voyage of discovery. Each day revealing new patterns of adaptation along England's transformed shoreline. The Wild Margin's data storage was reaching capacity when a message from Cass called them back to Whitby.

"The festival is all set for Saturday!" Cass wrote, their excitement palpable. "Enviroconnex have finished their study just in time to present their findings. The whole coast is talking about it. I can't wait to see you both." The message ended with a heart, a smiley face, and a string of retro flower emojis that made Rowan smile despite himself.

"We should check the gas platform sites one last time on the way," Ash said, studying the navigation display where their survey points glowed like stars in a constellation of data. Rowan nodded, marking coordinates on his Meridian. The old rigs had become artificial reefs, hosting complex ecosystems that were adapting to the warmer sea and changing current patterns.

That morning, the sea lay unusually still, a rare calm that seemed almost expectant. Through the Wild Margin's transparent hull, Rowan watched Ash swim among the complex ecosystem still thriving around the old gas platform legs. Hosting marine life that shouldn't be this far north. Ash moved effortlessly in the water, and Rowan wondered if there was anything she couldn't do? She is as graceful in water as she is on deck, he thought, in contrast to his own conscious clumsiness.

The warming had drawn species from southern waters, while the changing current patterns created new nutrient upwellings. The organisms had developed ways to handle the North Sea's increasingly unstable conditions, from storm-driven freshwater influxes to seasonal temperature extremes, creating stable micro-environments amid the chaos.

"Look at these connections," Ash said, studying the samples she'd collected. Her copper braid had come undone in the diving process, salt water making her hair curl around her face. "These samples are our best yet of cross species resilience."

Rowan found himself watching Ash as much as the samples. Over months at sea, she'd become far more than a research partner. Her methodical brilliance, her easy confidence, her way of connecting with people and ecosystems alike. But he hadn't found the courage to speak of it, to risk changing what they'd built together.

"I still don't really get it," he said instead, focusing back on the samples. "The melting ice and all the rain, it's diluting the salinity, right?" He hesitated, half-expecting Ash to be disappointed in his confusion. "So, the coastal plants that don't like salt are getting less salt from the tide, and the rain's washing it away from the soil, so I understand them being healthier. But the sea plants that do like salt seem to be thriving just as much."

"Look at this," Ash said, adjusting the microscope. Her voice changed when she talked about her discoveries – softer, almost reverent.

Rowan peered through the eyepiece. The cell structures blurred then snapped into focus, alien and familiar at once.

"They're regulating their internal chemistry," he said, understanding blooming. "Creating boundaries where none existed before."

"Yes, but that's not what keeps me awake at night." She switched samples with the practiced ease of someone who'd done this thousands of times. "It's this."

Rowan looked at the new slide.

"They're not just surviving side by side," she said, watching his face rather than the sample. "They're building highways between worlds that should never connect. Just like the land plants that Cass has studied."

The new image revealed delicate threads stretching between different cells – a gossamer highway.

"Like a chemical filtration system," Rowan mused, watching the microscopic connections between plant cells.

"And we're seeing genetic expressions activated that have been dormant for millennia," Ash continued, her excitement building. "Some of the coastal plants descended from marine ancestors that moved to land hundreds of millions of years ago. They're essentially reactivating ancient genetic pathways that their ancestors used in saltwater environments."

"You're saying they're remembering their evolutionary past?"

"In a way, yes. DNA carries the history of all adaptations, even those that haven't been expressed for aeons. Under the right stress conditions, these plants are accessing genetic toolkits, their species haven't used since before humans existed."

"So, this isn't invention," Rowan said thinking out loud, the insight Ash had shared still crystallising as he spoke. "They're just remembering."

Ash considered this; head tilted. She smiled self-consciously. "We're not really supposed to say it like that."

"Why not?"

"You know very well. Too mystical. Not proper science." She turned back to the microscope. "But I know what you mean, sometimes proper science just doesn't have the right words. If you can sum it all up, please feel free."

"I told you, I'm not a doctor. I just observe the Earth. I don't pretend to know how it works, it all seems weird lately."

Rowan thought of his mother's stories about the old ways, how she'd touch plants and talk to them with reverence, while his father rolled his eyes. He'd sided with his father then. Now he wasn't so sure.

"Nature doesn't need much opportunity," Ash said more gently. "It will make the most of every tiny chance to connect life and develop it. If humans had all just observed like you, instead of using everything... Our Mother Earth wouldn't be having to try this hard to make things right. Most of the time we're all just getting in the way."

The wind was picking up now and the temperature dropped noticeably. They needed to head for Whitby and get ready for the festival tomorrow. Reluctantly, they began securing their samples and equipment, preparing The Wild Margin for the journey back to port.

The first warning that the festival preparations might be interrupted came from the Lagrange space weather monitoring network. Everyone knew that the Solar Cycle was approaching its maximum, and the observatories positioned between Earth and Sun had been tracking increasing coronal activity all week. What Rowan didn't expect was the alert that vibrated his Meridian against his skin, its living components pulsing with unusual urgency. He expanded the device, watching as it projected detailed atmospheric data into the air before him: an initial solar flare was on its way to saturate their sensors – electromagnetic energy reaching Earth in minutes rather than hours. The Meridian's self-protecting circuitry was already shifting to autonomous mode. Preparing to maintain essential functions through the coming disruption. Its own system was adequately shielded, but the satellites and IoT devices in its network were a mix of new and older technology.

He warned Ash, but little could be done to protect their devices at such short notice.

As their instruments struggled to recover from the initial burst, a more urgent alert followed: a massive coronal mass ejection had launched directly toward Earth. The automated warning estimated the impact would be in hours rather than days – not nearly as big as the legendary, devastating Carrington Event – but moving with unprecedented speed.

"This will disrupt communications," Rowan said, already seeing glitches in their satellite feeds. "The festival will have trouble streaming, and..."

He stopped, noticing Ash's attention had shifted to the weather modelling outputs. The atmospheric pressure was dropping faster than any recent records showed. What had been a typical spring storm system they'd been watching had suddenly intensified, feeding on the unusually warm surface waters.

More concerning still, its predicted track was shifting, accelerated by changes in the jet stream that no one had quite mapped yet.

"Pull up the regional feeds," Ash called from the helm. The Wild Margin's screen flickered as Rowan complied, but the display was already showing signs of electromagnetic interference.

Ash radioed the coast guard, requesting real-time data while she put on her Helm helmet. Through the patchy transmission, they learned that Scarborough, the closest major port, was already preparing for the incoming storm. Its massive tidal barrier was lowering – standard protocol when storm systems threatened the historic town. With no prior clearance, they wouldn't be able to enter before it closed.

Ash's helmet connected, providing her with a clearer view than the struggling screens. The satellite system feeding it had clearly taken a beating from the flare, but it showed enough to confirm their options were limited. Robin Hood's Bay, North Landing and Boggle Hole would not provide adequate shelter in dangerous storm surge conditions. Bridlington was too far south, they'd be fighting the storm's leading edge all the way.

Their current position among the rusting towers of the old gas field suddenly felt precarious. The platforms' skeletal frames creaked in the building swell, and parts were known to fall during storms. The Wild Margin's helm system chimed another warning as wave heights increased.

"Whitby's our best chance," Ash said finally, studying the data with the focus that Rowan had come to admire. "They don't have a tidal barrier – it's a gate system. If we go now and move fast, we stand a good chance of slipping through before it fully closes." She didn't need to add that they'd be running before the storm, committed to their course once they started.

"At least they know we're coming," Rowan added, trying to sound more confident than he felt.

Dr Dahl's message arrived as they rushed to finish battening down the lab equipment – the Dutch designer responding to Ash's urgent query about his position. He had already safely arrived in Whitby harbour ahead of schedule, making good time on the crossing.

The message cut off as more electromagnetic disturbances hit. Rowan watched their communications array degrading in real time, followed by glitches in the navigation display. What he could still see clearly was the network of oceanographic buoys lighting up with storm warnings. He put his safety helmet on and checked that the communications link with Ash was working.

Rowan helped Ash get them underway, trying to ignore how his Meridian kept vibrating with warnings. Ash assured him her helmet view was stable enough to guide them safely.

"The festival will be nearly built by now," he said, thinking of all the work Cass and the others had put into the gathering. "All those temporary structures, visiting boats..."

A memory flashed, of their first storm together, the near disaster that had brought them closer. But they weren't the same people now. They were forewarned and prepared, and this remarkable boat that he'd come to understand had never let them down.

"Time to test some theoretical physics," Ash said, her voice steady as she engaged the hydrofoil system to its maximum extension.

The Wild Margin lifted, finding its balance between air and water. They'd engaged the foils countless times, but never this far out, through fear of damaging a precious sea creature, like that beautiful whale, with the blade-like structures. But now she had no choice.

Targeting the fastest route to Whitby, they caught the first real taste of the storm's energy, gale force winds that could either drive them home or tear them apart. The boat's solar skin automatically adjusted, each panel finding the optimal angle to harvest what light remained while minimising drag. The hull hummed with power as they accelerated, skimming above the growing waves with the motors running at maximum capacity.

Back in Whitby, Isaac's struggling screen lit up with alerts from the ocean monitoring network. The incoming data made his blood pressure rise, this wasn't like recent storms.

Before he could even begin organising a response, he found Mae already mobilising the community in the Hall with Cass. Her decades of coastal life had taught her to read the signs before any official warnings.

"The Wild Margin's out there," Cass told Isaac, while trying frantically to check messages but finding no signal. "They were out at the rigs earlier..."

Bramley circled anxiously between them, sensing the change in atmosphere. His mismatched heritage showed in the way he moved, the border collie instinct to herd them to safety, mixed with something less structured and fearful. He pressed against Cass's leg, offering silent support.

"Go back and get them on the radio, Isaac," Mae ordered, her calm authority cutting through the growing tension. "He'll look after them now, Cass. I need you focused here."

"Bram stay." Mae asserted, "He calms the children, Isaac. Let him stay."

"Aye," Isaac obeyed as he headed for the door. Bramley trotted faithfully behind, but Mae closed the door between them.

Isaac found Dr Dahl helping to secure the festival structures.

"I could use your help," he said to the Dutch designer. "Tell me more about Ash's vessel, what speed can it handle in storm conditions?"

The festival setup was transforming quickly around them in preparation for the lethal winds to come. Regina and the

Enviroconnex team had also found themselves being integrated into the community's practiced protocols – corporate hierarchies suddenly irrelevant in the face of immediate need. Isaac could see Regina was not amused and just wanted to leave.

Dr Dahl was still talking to Isaac in the harbour master's office when Regina marched in, her corporate composure visibly cracking. She'd been trying to arrange evacuation for her team, but nothing was working as expected.

"What do you mean, 'cancelled'?" she demanded, her voice rising an octave.

Behind her, the Enviroconnex team huddled around their devices, each finding the same lack of signal – an unheard-of situation for their generation. Their sleek autonomous transport sat useless on the landing pad above the harbour, its AI refusing to override safety protocols.

"Can somebody here fly us out, please?" Regina barked in Dr Dahl's direction, mistaking his calm demeanour and badge covered jacket for piloting experience.

"Even if you could fly your thing manually," Isaac said, looking up at the pad normally reserved for the Air Ambulance, "you wouldn't be in the air for very long. This storm that's coming will chew you up and spit you out. Your exit window closed twenty minutes ago, unless you want to walk home." The old fisherman's tone held none of his usual warmth. These were the same corporate types who'd once dismissed his fish stock predictions as "anecdotal evidence," ignoring the obvious decline that had decimated coastal livelihoods.

Dr Ghadah, seeing her employer's rising panic, stepped forward.

"Perhaps we should focus on how we can help?" she suggested, practical even in crisis. "I'm happy to carry equipment or secure structures."

The lights flickered as the building's emergency power kicked in. Mae appeared in the doorway, her quiet authority immediately drawing all eyes.

"We need hands to secure the event space," she said simply. Her gaze swept over the corporate visitors with neither judgment nor deference. "If everyone works, everyone's safe. We can all eat together in the hall tonight. Everyone's welcome if they pull their weight."

Regina looked at her team – their technology failing, their digital authority suddenly meaningless in a world that required immediate physical action. Something shifted in her expression, a calculation giving way to something more human.

"What do you need us to do?"

As they followed Mae out into the strengthening wind, Regina glimpsed what she thought was the Wild Margin safe in the harbour. It was actually Dr Dahl's vessel – the Zeevaarder, already secured in the inner harbour. The Dutch designer, whom she had just met without recognising, was supposed to showcase the prototype at the festival. A demonstration that would now have to wait.

Out at sea, Rowan and Ash were learning what the Wild Margin could really do when pushed to its limits. The hull flexed as another wave crashed. Hydrofoils whistled, adjusting to building seas, sound rising to a banshee wail that set Rowan's teeth on edge.

"Storm's moving faster," he announced, stating what was becoming painfully obvious with each passing minute.

Ash nodded, her focus absolute.

"We'll have one chance at the harbour entrance..." She didn't need to finish. They both knew the stakes: miscalculate and they'd slam into the harbour gates or shatter against unyielding stone.

The deck pitched. Rowan grabbed the console rail, knuckles white.

The boat's hull flexed again as another wave lifted them, sensors and structure working in concert to maintain stability. Through breaks in the spray, they caught glimpses of Whitby's skyline, the great abbey ruins stark against steel-grey clouds.

"Not far now," Ash called over the comms, her voice steady despite the strain evident in her posture.

The deck pitched violently as a rogue wave caught them broadside. Rowan flinched, but his attention never left his duties. Strange how terror and exhilaration could feel so similar, he thought fleetingly, channelling his adrenaline into focused action.

The hydrofoils sang a high, changing note as he adjusted their length. Not full retraction – they needed some lift – but angled to keep them stable in the increasingly chaotic wave patterns. All those hours Ash had spent teaching him these system limits, now made visceral sense. The physics of speed and survival.

He felt her brief touch on his shoulder, a gesture that carried more meaning than either of them had yet discussed. Even in crisis, her movements were reassuring. The Wild Margin responded like a living thing under her guidance – an extension of her will as much as her experience.

"I'm good," Rowan said with a grateful smile, his attention remaining on his duties.

A massive swell lifted their stern. Ash's hands controlled the wheel with intuitive precision, anticipating the boat's movement rather than reacting to it.

"We'll need full power through the centre channel," she called, her voice tight with concentration.

The Wild Margin's systems flashed warnings as they pushed past thirty-five knots. The electric motors were running dangerously hot, well beyond their rated capacity. Through salt-stung eyes, Rowan watched their speed climb: thirty-seven... thirty-eight...

There was nothing for him to do now but hold position and trust Ash's judgment. She would let him know if she needed him; until then, he wouldn't break her concentration with unnecessary words.

Through the spray, the harbour entrance took shape – two massive composite gates sliding from their housings as the storm surge triggered automatic protocols. Ash's helm visor outlined them with a crisp green line, tracking their movement clearly.

"Helm, status report," Ash commanded through her visor mic.

"Multiple systems compromised," the AI responded. "Recommend reducing speed."

Rowan adjusted his own safety helmet. "We've lost most instruments," he reported, his voice steady despite his racing heart. "I think the sail controls are completely fried."

"We'll have to do this ourselves then," Ash said, making a decision with the same swift certainty that had drawn him to her from the beginning. "Helm, disengage safety protocols."

"Warning: recommended parameters exceeded."

"Helm, manual override."

"Override confirmed."

They'd need everything the Wild Margin could give them, even beyond its programmed limits. Through her visor, Ash tracked the gates' closing sequence, calculating their narrowing window of opportunity. The boat's systems might be failing, but with Rowan handling the sails and her helmet giving her a clear view of the wave dynamics, they had a chance – if she could squeeze just a little more speed from the straining vessel.

"Can you keep the gates open a little longer, Isaac?" Dr Dahl asked, watching the Wild Margin's approach through high-powered binoculars.

"They're sensor activated. There's an override, but we'll not get them closed again before the swell follows Ash in." Isaac's face was grim as he made the calculation. "I'll tell the lifeboat crew to suit up."

"Original plan's still good," Ash told Rowan, though her tone lacked conviction. "We'll slim down, retract the foils as we go in."

But even as she said it, Rowan's eyes were tracking the gates' movement with growing trepidation. They were closing too fast, a narrowing canyon between the jaws of a mechanical leviathan. Ash was making the same calculations he was, and the gate outline in her visor had turned to flashing red.

The Wild Margin screamed toward the harbour gap at forty knots. "We're not going to make it," Rowan said, watching their only passage to safety shrinking with alarming speed.

Ash's hands were already moving across the controls. "New plan!" she shouted, her voice holding a conviction that steadied him. "Keep the foils extended. More speed." She shot him a quick look, eyes visible through her visor, holding his gaze for just a moment. "We're going to jump, okay?"

Rowan's stomach lurched as he understood. "Okay," he gasped, the word catching in his throat.

"Get ready to raise the keel."

"Get those sails configured, we'll need lift at the bow."

They worked with the practiced synchronisation of months at sea. Rowan's hands found the sheets in the growing darkness, adjusting the trim until he felt the perfect tension that would provide maximum lift without tearing the sails from their mounts.

They'd need full speed from both motor and sails, precisely when the keel came up, a manoeuvre that would sacrifice stability for the chance to clear the barrier. The thought made Rowan's knees weak, but there was no time for fear. The storm's energy drove them forward. He could feel it in his bones – the vibration through the deck, the hydrofoils trembling on the edge of cavitation.

"Ready on the jib!" Ash's command cut through the howling wind.

This was taking danger to yet another level. More sail area meant more drive, but one wrong gust could tear the solar sail away completely. Rowan worked the lines with practiced precision, feeling as much as seeing the sail's shape in the fading light. His fingers ached, wet and cold, his fingerless gloves providing little comfort against the elements.

Too much belly and they'd lose speed, too flat and they'd risk a catastrophic gybe that could capsize them instantly.

The Wild Margin accelerated again, hydrofoils whistling, engines hurling them forward. Forty-five knots now, the storm front a dark wall behind them, running them down like a stampede. Each wave that caught them felt like it might tear the vessel in half, but somehow the hull kept flexing, kept holding together.

"Halyard tension!" Ash called. Rowan adjusted instantly, working with her as if they were a single organism.

Through his binoculars, Isaac could see them approaching through the rain. They were closing fast, riding waves that would have swamped a conventional vessel. The solar sails were trimmed to extreme angles, somehow holding together as Ash and Rowan pushed physics to its limits.

Dr Dahl watched the closing gates, his face etched with concern. The Margin was his design, his knowledge – being tested beyond limits. His heart pounded with a deep sense of foreboding.

On the Wild Margin's deck, time seemed to compress into heartbeats. No words needed now, they'd learned to read each other like wind and water, like the interconnected life they'd been studying all these months.

Through the spray, the harbour gates – mighty barriers standing at least fifteen feet above the water line, designed to protect everything behind them that they'd grown to love. The gap between them had narrowed to perhaps 16 feet now. Not enough time to slip their twenty-foot beam through now, even if they'd kept to their original plan.

Behind them, the storm front was reaching for them with great, dark claws. Ahead lay the shelter of home.

They were running faster than their own bow wave now, the boat's entire form trying to break free from the water that had birthed its design.

"Trim!" Ash called.

"Keel retraction?" Rowan responded, hand poised over the control that would sacrifice their stability for a chance to fly.

Ash's eyes never left the helm's view of the approaching gates, reading the waves, the wind, the precise moment when all forces would align. "Not yet... not yet..."

A massive swell lifted their stern. This was their wave – their one chance to convert forward momentum into lift.

Ash turned to meet Rowan's eyes. "Now!"

Rowan slammed the keel retractor. The Wild Margin shuddered as the deep stabiliser pulled away. For a heartbeat, they balanced on the edge of chaos – sails straining, hydrofoils screaming, hull trembling with the effort of defying gravity.

Up in Mae's cottage, Cass pressed against the window, desperate for a glimpse of the returning vessel. "I need to see..." They ran toward the door, unable to bear the waiting any longer.

"You need to help me with these children," Mae stepped in firmly, though her eyes remained gentle. She understood – they all had someone they loved outside. The children's parents were lifeboat crew, preparing to show the storm no fear. "Please, Cass, show them your drawings. Keep them busy for me."

The keel was not designed to retract fully, so Ash knew they must aim for the last remaining opening to slip it through as they ramped the hull over. The foils would never retract in time, but with enough lift from the sails, they might just clear the top of the gates.

Isaac knew it was too late – they could not make it through now. "They've missed their chance. We need to launch the lifeboat."

"Wait!" Dr Dahl grabbed Isaac's arm as he recognised what they were attempting. "They're going to jump it."

"Holy hell, no!" Isaac gasped.

On board, Rowan made the decision for her. "Ash, do it now!" he shouted, the gates' dark wall looming before them like the end of all things.

Isaac and Dahl ran outside into the wind and rain, unable to look away from what was about to happen.

Then physics caught the vessel perfectly. A great wave's energy translated through the hydrofoils into pure lift, while the angled sails pulled their bow skyward. The Wild Margin's fifty-foot length quivered as the wide beam caught the wind.

The tilting deck thrust up beneath their feet as the boat broke free of the waves entirely. For one impossible moment, they were airborne.

Spray hung in the air around them. Rowan felt his stomach clench, his hands losing grip on the rope. He grabbed instinctively for Ash's life preserver, needing something, anything to anchor him as the world fell away. Their harnesses held them against the wind in the suspended seconds between sea and sky.

Isaac and Dr Dahl stood awestruck on the harbour wall, witnessing this death defying-gambit. The massive gates locked together below the flying vessel, indifferent to the drama playing out above.

For a moment that stretched like eternity, the boat hung like a leaping salmon, water sluicing from the streaming hull in silver sheets. In that suspended heart-beat, Rowan clung to Ash, everything they'd never said to each other compressed into what might be their final moment together.

Then physics reasserted itself with vengeance.

The deck fell away beneath them. Impact came with a crash so violent it shocked the air from their lungs. The keel housing twisted against the harbour gate, hydraulics screaming. Warning lights flashed unseen as compart-ment bulkheads sealed automatically.

Ash lost control of the helm, the impact wrenching the wheel from her hands.

The starboard hydrofoil reconnected with the water first, composite materials shearing away as it hit the surface. The Wild Margin's hull flexed as designed, spreading the impact through its structure rather than concentrating it at any single point of failure.

Their feet rejoined the deck with merciless force, the shock driving them to their knees. They slid down the saturated deck, slamming against the console. Seawater exploded to engulf them, as they plunged deep into the harbour's chop, then shot back through the surface like a cork from a bottle.

"They did it," Dr Dahl shouted with excited relief. "They actually..." He turned to Isaac, but the old fisherman was already moving, in emergency response.

The Wild Margin lay in the water, trailing pieces of sophisticated skin, proud technology humbled by elemental forces. But the core hull held, and inside, the crew huddled together, alive against all odds.

Dahl jumped aboard and caught a line from Isaac. Crew from other boats joined in to get the tattered vessel to the wall. Behind them, the storm surge hit the gates with titanic force. White water exploded high into the air, some spilling over the top, raising a swell in the harbour. But the gates stood strong against nature's wrath.

The lifeboat crew arrived, relieved to find a rescue mission had become a recovery operation. They jumped aboard to tend to Ash and Rowan.

Dr Dahl secured his damaged creation, his quick fingers finding the essential ties while leaving damage assessment for tomorrow. The Wild Margin's broken solar skin fluttered and slapped against the hull in the wind, a beautiful design brought down but not defeated.

Ash and Rowan were carried off the boat on stretchers. "Get inside, all of you!" Isaac shouted over the wind. The Harbour Master's office was closest, its reinforced windows rattling with each new gust. They struggled across the dock in groups, holding each other upright against the storm's fury, the brightly suited lifeboat crew forming a protective wall around the injured couple.

Inside, they dripped onto ancient floorboards while Isaac kept one ear on the radio, listening to the coastguard communications. Ash squeezed water from her hair, her trusted hands now shaking uncontrollably. Tears of relief joined the saltwater on her cheeks. Rowan found himself watching her, half-waking from a surreal daze, still not fully processing his new surroundings. When Ash caught his eye, something passed between them – a recognition that they still had each other, that against all odds, they were alive.

"Your head is bleeding," Ash said with alarm, seeing the dark red blood running down Rowan's face.

With that, the crew lifted him away for treatment.

"Don't worry, Ash, he's a strong lad," Isaac said reassuringly, and with that, he left, whisking Rowan away with three of the crew.

Ash sat with Dr Dahl as the remaining rescue team checked her over and treated her minor injuries. Once they had finished, they wrapped a silver thermal blanket around her shoulders and left to rejoin their families. Ash stayed with Dahl, speculating about the damage to their beloved vessel. She felt bruised but safe now, nestled within this resilient community that had taken her in as one of their own.

"First light," Dahl said quietly, patting her shoulder. "Nothing more to be done tonight except stay safe and rest."

Soon Isaac returned in his rain-soaked oilskins. "Mae's got soup warming at the hall. Best we all head there now before this gets any worse."

Through the darkness, the storm drew its full strength around Whitby's walls. The harbour gates took the brunt of it, their composite structure resonating with each impact. Tomorrow they would assess damage, begin repairs, examine what they'd learned. But tonight was for warmth, for community, and for the quiet knowledge that against the odds, everyone had made it home.

CHAPTER 7

CASSIOPEIA RISING

D awn crept through the community hall's windows, painting patterns on sleeping bags arranged in neat rows across the floor. The storm's fury had faded to a distant grumble, leaving behind the familiar sound of seagulls returning to the harbour, their cries a testament to survival and continuity.

Rowan woke to find Ash already up, sitting quietly with Dr Dahl near the hall's entrance. He recognised the story she was telling, about the coastal community near Flamborough Head, where children had developed their own wonderful names for the new hybrid plants emerging in the tidal zones. The Dutch designer listened with genuine interest, his weathered face lighting up at each imaginative detail.

Rowan watched them, savouring the quiet scene. Ash had a bandage on her ankle where she must have sprained it during their landing, and her elbow was red and grazed. His own injuries felt minor in comparison to what might have been – just two stitches beside his left eye where he'd struck the control panel just below his helmet line during impact.

He didn't want to disturb her; she was happy with other people now. He spotted the side door and decided to slip away, give her space. What he felt for her, words could not do justice, and this was not the place.

He sat up carefully, his body protesting with a symphony of aches. Everything hurt – muscles, joints, even his teeth seemed to ache. But he was alive. They both were. The miracle of that fact washed over him anew.

Ash caught his movement and looked over, her face breaking into a smile of such genuine warmth that something shifted permanently inside him. She murmured something to Dahl and made her way across the hall, navigating between sleeping forms, with a limp that clearly pained her.

"How's the head?" she asked softly, sitting beside him.

"Better than it deserves to be," he replied, trying to ignore how his pulse quickened at her proximity. "How's the Wild Margin?"

Her eyes clouded slightly. "Still afloat. Dahl says most of the damage is repairable, though the hydrofoils are a write-off. We'll know more once we can look properly."

Around them, the hall stirred gradually to life. Members of Regina's team emerged from their bags and blankets, looking surprisingly human, their corporate polish softened by a night spent sharing storm stories with the community. The experience had transformed them somehow, breaking down barriers that no amount of formal outreach could have achieved.

Mae was already organising breakfast, moving through the hall with quiet efficiency. Her ancient kettle's whistle drew people like a beacon, some of the younger city dwellers examining it with curiosity, never having seen one outside of a museum.

Rowan struggled to his feet, new injuries announced themselves sharply as he attempted to straighten. "I need to check on our samples," he said, remembering the precious cargo they'd risked so much to bring home.

"Dr Dahl already secured the lab for us," Ash assured him, helping him find his balance. "The hull integrity held – everything inside should be fine."

But Rowan needed to go, his emotions were too strong to be beside her. "I still want to see. I'll be fine on my own."

Ash nodded, understanding without explanation. "Go on then, I'll join you when I've had some breakfast. Do you want me to bring you some, when I'm done?"

"No, I'll do myself a drink later, I'm fine." He wasn't but he wanted some space. Part of him wanted to throw his arms around her, while another wanted to run and hide. What if she didn't feel the same? If he crossed that line and the question was asked, he knew they could never go back to what they'd had.

The morning light revealed both destruction and re-silience as he made his way to the harbour. The surge gates had performed admirably, protecting the inner basin from the worst of the storm's fury. The festival's temporary structures showed clear damage but remained largely intact, their modular design proving more resilient than traditional rigid constructions.

The Wild Margin lay in emergency mooring, its proud lines now humbled. One hydrofoil hung twisted and mangled, the other completely gone. The solar skin showed patches of damage where the impact had overwhelmed even the biomimetic design. Yet the core hull had held, protecting both crew and cargo through their desperate leap of faith.

Once inside, Rowan surveyed the damage to the lab. The initial chaos wasn't as bad as he'd feared, most equipment had been properly secured before their race home. The microscope had suffered irreparable damage, but the sample storage remained intact. Their precious cargo of evidence had survived.

He began to pick through the mess methodically, restoring order with flowing efficiency. Before long, the lab was taking shape again, each item finding its place in their well-established system.

"Still floating, I see," came Dr Dahl's voice from the doorway. The Dutch designer climbed carefully aboard, his experienced eyes already assessing damage points. "You were very lucky last night."

"Oh, I know," Rowan admitted, guilt washing over him. "It was foolish and reckless, and I'm so sorry we damaged your beautiful vessel, Doctor."

"Yes, next time please jump higher!" Dahl laughed, the sound incongruous in the damaged cabin. He moved to the deck, running expert hands over the fractured systems. "I'll be back when I've spoken to the boatyard," he called as he left, already formulating repair plans in his mind.

Rowan had nearly finished restoring order when Ash joined him.

"Looking good!" she exclaimed. "I was..." She trailed off as she caught sight of her crushed microscope. "Oh, that's not good."

"Everything else is fine," he assured her. "I'll get you a new one, a better one."

"Silly man," she said with a fond smile that made his chest tighten. "I'll get it fixed."

They worked through the morning cataloguing samples and assessing damages. Hardly speaking, as small talk seemed more like avoidance than communication.

The specimens from the gas rig were mostly intact – delicate evidence of nature's adaptation preserved. Each organism told part of a larger story of life responding to change at micro and macro levels.

Dahl returned near noon. "We can fabricate replacement foils here – your community workshop has the capability," he announced. "The solar skin will self-repair once we stabilise the torn sections. But we'll have to lift the hull to replace the keel housing. They can't do that till Monday."

"Can it ever really be the same again?" Ash asked, a note of sadness in her voice.

"No," he said simply, then smiled. "That would not be very progressive, would it?" He laughed as he headed off again to source more advanced components than the originals.

"Is he always like this?" Rowan asked.

"Yep, he's funny and I love it." Ash beamed a grin. Rowan wondered if he should be funnier as she tended to laugh more at him than with him.

By the afternoon, Rowan was flagging, his bruised body aching as he tidied the galley and searched for something to eat. Through the portholes, he could see the festival being rebuilt with remarkable speed. Everyone was working together – local residents, festival participants, even the Enviroconnex team had shed their corporate attire for practical work clothes.

Cass stood surrounded by a group that included several Enviroconnex interns, all deep in animated conversation. Mae directed community members arriving with bicycle trailers loaded with crafted items, baskets of food, and potted plants for the exhibition areas. The smell of baked bread and spicy cooking began to waft across the harbour.

"Would you care to join me for lunch, sir?" Ash asked with a playful formality as she hobbled into the galley, her hair tied back in a fresh braid.

"I'd love to, but I can't crawl very far," Rowan admitted with a wince.

"We'll limp along together," she laughed, offering her arm.

They had barely made it to the dock when Regina approached with Dr Ghadah. The mighty consortium boss looked different, her usually perfect appearance somewhat dishevelled, but her eyes clearer somehow, more present.

"You know," Regina said, turning to the Doctor, her voice carrying very little of its former corporate edge, "this is exactly the kind of adaptation we need to document. Not just the biological changes, but how communities respond, how technology evolves." She looked at the rebuilding effort with something like wonder. "I may write a paper on it."

"Your community network has produced some interesting correlations with Dr Ghadah's formal findings," she continued, turning to Rowan. "The patterns we're seeing in the official data set, match what your observers have been documenting all along."

Rowan exchanged glances with Ash, surprised by this unexpected validation.

"It's nice to see you too, Regina," he said with mild sarcasm, managing a tired smile.

"Would you like to come aboard?" Ash offered. "Once we've eaten, I'll happily show you what we found at the platforms."

"The lab has survived remarkably well," Regina observed as they entered, not knowing they'd spent all morning restoring it.

Dr Ghadah followed, her sharp eyes taking in the carefully organised samples and documentation system they'd developed. This was clearly not the haphazard citizen science she'd been expecting.

"Your methodology is unorthodox, but the results you've been sharing..." Regina began, then hesitated. "Your community network has produced some fascinating data about coastal ecosystem development. Each location slightly different, but all showing similar patterns of mutual support."

"Because we're working with people who watch these changes every day," Ash explained, pulling up their integrated database on a working monitor. "Combining their knowledge with systematic observation. Mae's garden plots are like living laboratories, showing us how species adapt in relationship rather than in isolation."

"We've identified the same adaptation patterns, just through different analytical frameworks," Dr Ghadah confirmed. "Our instruments measure what your observers experience directly. Combined, the picture becomes much clearer."

"The consortium is discussing a new initiative," Regina said carefully, revealing plans on her Meridian. "A formal partnership between institutional and community research. Properly funded, but..." she smiled slightly, "perhaps with fewer lengthy consultations and more direct engagement."

Through the porthole, behind her, Rowan could see Cass showing the Enviroconnex junior researchers their field documentation. The teenager moved with newfound confidence, guiding professionals with natural authority.

"We'd need to maintain the network's independence," Rowan said, still watching Cass with quiet pride. "Keep the focus on practical observation rather than institutional metrics."

"That's exactly what we're proposing," Dr Ghadah replied, surprising them both. "Understanding environmental change requires multiple ways of seeing, maintained over extended periods. Your citizen observers provide continuity and context that formal research visits simply cannot match."

Regina switched to a new view of the plans. "We're calling it the Coastal Adaptation Network," she explained. "A series of research nodes designed to combine community observation with institutional resources. Not imposing laboratories, but living spaces where different forms of knowledge can meet and grow." She gestured at the harbour around them, where the community worked together in practiced coordination. "Rather like what we're seeing here."

"So, are you interested in leading this project or not, Rowan?" Regina asked with a hint of her old impatience returning. "We need someone who understands both worlds."

Rowan thought about his old signal station, isolated on its hill. Then he felt the Wild Margin under his feet, battered but healing. The growing network on the dockside working as one. He realised he didn't miss his old life at all – the solitude, the distance, the safety of watching from afar.

"I think the best person for this job is just out there," he said, pointing to Cass, who was demonstrating a soil sampling technique to an attentive audience. "They've already built the network from the ground up. They understand the science, the community, and the purpose better than anyone."

"I'll second that," Ash said enthusiastically, her hand finding his.

"Your plans are amazing," Rowan continued, "and we can definitely support everything you're suggesting. But Cass is the leader you need."

"But now if you'll excuse us," Ash added, pulling Rowan gently toward the door, "we need to eat before we fall over. Feel free to stay and look around, Doctor."

As they limped down the dock together, Rowan felt something settle inside him, a decision made without words. Wherever the Wild Margin sailed next, he would be aboard, if Ash would have him.

Back onboard, Dr Dahl had returned, he was frowning at the helm's diagnostic panel. "Are the happy couple in?" Mae asked as she looked in behind him. "I brought them a hot snack."

"No, sorry Mae, I think that's what they've gone to find."

"Have you eaten?" Mae asked, holding out a hot pasty.

"Not since breakfast."

"Well, you have this, and I'll put one in the galley, they'll be glad of it later."

"How's the repairs going?" Mae asked, returning from the galley to find Dr Dahl frowning again.

"The physical damage we can repair, but the Wild Margin's adaptivity protocols are compromised. The system's refusing to integrate the new configurations."

"So, the boat doesn't recognise itself anymore?" Mae asked curiously, her eyes taking in the displays.

"I think I read somewhere, that symbiotic intelligence systems protect themselves from what they perceive as anomalous structural patterns." She continued.

She approached the console, her hands hovering over the interface with unexpected familiarity.

"May I?"

Dr Dahl hesitated, then stepped aside with a curious nod. Mae's old fingers moved fluently, navigating through layers of code in the Wild Margin's systems.

"You're familiar with biomimetic intelligence architecture," Dahl observed, his tone a careful mix of surprise and professional interest.

"I've encountered similar systems," Mae replied, attention focused on the screen. "Your design is elegant – the neural adaptation protocols especially." She pulled up a visualisation showing the vessel's self-perception. "See here? It's trying to protect itself by rejecting what it sees as damaging interventions. But it needs to recognise the difference between the repair and threat."

Rather than overriding the protocols, Mae began adjusting them, adding parameters that would allow the system to recognise emerging patterns while still maintaining safeguards.

"How did you know to do that?" Dahl asked when the system finally accepted the new configuration.

"Complex adaptive systems follow certain principles," Mae said, stepping back from the console. "Like recognising the difference between disorder and emergent order." She glanced at the now-functioning display. "Your vessel is impressive work, Dr Dahl. It's learning to think like an ecosystem."

"That was the goal," Dahl acknowledged. "Your understanding of synthetic intelligence protocols is quite extraordinary."

"Well, there was a time when I believed in saving the world through code... but not all battles are meant to be fought in the light." Mae smiled. "I'm just a lucky amateur Doctor, I read a lot at home. Cass and Isaac always have something that needs fixing. And the garden teaches similar lessons about adaptation, just at a more advanced organic level than I will ever understand."

As she left, Dahl looked thoughtfully at the code modifications she'd made – elegant solutions that somehow seemed familiar, reminiscent of the foundational adaptive algorithms, published years ago. Mae certainly was well-read.

Later, as Ash and Rowan made their way back, admiring the stalls, Cass hurried over, their expression a mix of excitement and concern.

"There's a news crew coming," they said in a rush. "The Yorkshire Post heard about what we're doing, and they're sending reporters tomorrow. Isaac's really worried it'll bring unwanted attention."

Sure enough, the old fisherman was gesturing emphatically to Mae by the harbour wall, his weather-beaten face creased with worry.

"I'll just keep out of their way," Mae said. "We don't need outsiders turning this into a spectacle," he was saying as they approached. "Bad enough with corporate vultures circling. I bet this was Regina's idea."

Rowan glanced at Ash, surprised to find himself about to take the opposite view.

"I think it might be a good thing," he said, drawing startled looks from the others. "The news is really designed to tell us when to duck and cover these days. They have so much bad climate news that they barely have time for a good news story. It's good that they're taking an interest"

Mae's eyes creased with focus. "You think we're good news, then?"

"I know we are," Rowan replied with conviction that surprised even himself. "People are anxious after what's happened to their land, anxious about their children's future. The reality is there are loads of good people turning their climate anxiety into action, working with nature like you. If people knew about it, they might come and join in too."

He looked around at the rebuilding effort. "Let the journalists see what's happening here. Let them tell the world that nature is regenerating, and they're invited to come and help it."

Isaac looked unconvinced, but Mae nodded slowly.

"He's got a fair point. We need more hands, more eyes. More people to care about what happens next."

"Besides," Ash added with a smile, "I'd rather they report on how we're adapting than just show another depressing drone shot of a flooded town."

Cass's expression brightened. "I could show them around! Take them to talk to people."

"That would be great Cass," Rowan said, watching as even Isaac's resistance began to soften. "Let them see how we're building something new, not just mourning what we've lost."

CHAPTER 8

CONNECT AND THRIVE

N oah Ecosystems' London headquarters stood in stark contrast to Whitby's organic community growth. The carbon-negative tower featured living walls and precision-grown structural bamboo, yet something about its sleek design felt extractive rather than regenerative.

Inside the executive conference room, Co-Founding Director Maya Chowdhury studied the coastal adaptation data with growing concern. Unlike her colleagues who saw only commercial potential, she recognised something more profound occurring.

"These communities don't appear to be just documenting adaptation," Maya said, pointing to the Consortium's reports. "They're participating in it. The knowledge they're collecting may not be separable from the relationships they're building."

Aadan Zhao barely glanced up from his projections.

"The science is what matters, Maya. The community context is merely... incidental."

"That's dangerously reductive thinking," she countered. "What if the context is central to the value? The particular regenerative practices of the coastal communities, may be the very thing that has enabled these ecosystem developments?"

"We're not anthropologists and we don't sell training, so that's nice but irrelevant Maya."

"Maybe a bit of anthropology training would teach you to be less rude," Maya said with a frustrated frown. "I'm just saying that they are clearly doing something right, and just because it works there, doesn't mean it will work anywhere else, if the human impact element is different."

Aadan leaned forward, his voice dropping.

"Look, I believe in what they're doing too. But these adaptation patterns could help farming communities across three continents. They could transform food security for millions. But those millions don't want to hear about changing their ways, they just want a product, and they'll pay for it."

Maya studied him, recognising some sincerity beneath his corporate polish.

"So, we're going to patent it, package it, and price it beyond the reach of those who need it most. When this community could potentially teach the world to adapt for free? We should find a way to support them."

A look of irritation crossed Aadan's face.

"You know I've pushed for accessible licensing models. But we can't distribute what we can't develop, and development at scale requires investment." He tapped the financial projections. "This community approach is commendable, I'll grant you that. But it doesn't scale. It can't, and we're not a charity. I don't see you rushing to give them your dividends"

The board chair, Victor Chen, rolled his eyes. Twenty years running Noah had taught him to recognise when competing visions were both partially right, and these heated debates between Aadan and Maya were nothing new.

"Maya may have a good point about the community's part in these developments, and there may not be any replicable product to invest in here. We need to understand more before we commit. But Aadan's right to point out that localised solutions won't address global problems." He sighed. "The moment we announce our interest publicly, shareholders will demand immediate return on investment, ethics be damned. And if we don't engage, someone else will – someone who won't even have this conversation, before exploiting this opportunity."

He glanced between them. "Let's gather more information before committing. Aadan, take a small team to Whitby. Assess both the technical and social dimensions."

Maya stood.

"Take Vega. Their integrative analysis capabilities might help you see patterns you'd otherwise miss."

Aadan frowned but nodded. As Noah's most advanced synthetic citizen, Vega's observational protocols were unmatched, though their tendency toward independent conclusions occasionally frustrated him.

After the others had filed out, Maya remained, staring through the glass wall at London's redeveloped shoreline below – engineered coastal defences that had cost billions and would still eventually fail.

"You didn't say much after your initial objection," Victor noted, joining her.

"What's there to say? The quarterly projections speak louder than I ever could."

"I know you think I've sold out," Victor said quietly. "That I've forgotten why we started all this."

Maya turned to face him. "I actually think we're all trapped in a performance. We're playing sustainability while delivering shareholder value. Pretending we can have both when the metrics only really measure one thing that they care about."

"And yet," Victor gestured to the display wall showing Noah's global projects, "real work is happening. Damage restored. Carbon captured. Seeds preserved."

"Permissible innovation." She countered.

"Yes," Victor admitted. "But it's something. And what happens if groups like this coastal network expose the gap between our marketing and our reality? What happens to the thousands employed in our environmental teams when the funding dries up? What happens to the current projects? They may be insufficient, but they're still better than nothing?"

Maya noticed the lines etched around his eyes were deeper than when they'd founded Noah.

"Sometimes I wonder," Victor said, almost to himself, "if maintaining the positive narrative, is the most responsible choice we have. Not because it's good enough, but because the alternative is paralysis."

"Or transformation," Maya replied. "Which is what I see happening in these coastal communities. They're evolving new ways of working, openly, honestly."

"Evolution is messy, Maya. It leaves casualties." Victor gathered his materials. "And I've got a thousand employees, who can't afford to be among them."

Later, Maya briefed Vega privately, choosing her words carefully. "There's something special happening in these coastal communities. Something that might not fit our standard business models."

"My observation protocols prioritise accuracy over conformity to expectations," Vega assured her.

"Good." She hesitated. "When you're there... watch for the relationships, not just the mechanisms. Some things are worth protecting, even from ourselves."

As Maya left, Vega's processing systems flagged an anomaly, a slight priority shift in response to her words. Something about this mission felt resonant in ways their analy-

sis couldn't fully explain. The coastal community await-
ing them might offer more than just data to harvest.

In the following days, Whitby's first Coastal Science
Festival emerged from the storm's aftermath like the
plants they studied – adaptable, resilient, transformed.
Instead of conference halls and formal presentations,
knowledge flowed through Mae's expanded garden plots,
around the community observation stations, and aboard
redundant fishing boats, that would now be refitted as
floating laboratories under Regina's new plan and Cass's
leadership. Inspired by the Wild Margin's lab design.

By the time the Yorkshire Post journalists arrived, the
community had prepared a tour with Cass, that showed
both the challenges they faced and the ingenious ways
they were responding. The reporters, who had arrived not
expecting much of a story, left with a template for hope
that could be replicated in communities up and down the
coast.

"I wasn't sure about this press business," Isaac admitted to Rowan as they watched the journalists interviewing Regina about her plans. But seeing the way they've
been listening to the young ones – maybe you were right."

"Sometimes we need to be seen to be understood,"
Rowan replied, thinking of how much his own perspective had changed, since leaving his isolated tower. "Connection works both ways. It's a shame Mae didn't speak
to them, but Cass has done a really good job."

No sooner had the news team gone, when a sleek corporate transport descended onto Whitby harbour, bearing the unmistakable logo of Noah Ecosystems, the consortium's largest commercial partner.

"They weren't invited," Regina muttered, watching the craft land with obvious tension. "The board must have told them."

"Who are they?" Cass asked, noticing how the atmosphere among the consortium staff had shifted from collaborative to anxious, as a tall figure disembarked.

"Aadan Zhao. Head of biotech products." Said Dr Ghadah. "They've been pushing for exclusive commercialisation rights to any 'applicable discoveries' from our research," her fingers made air quotes around the corporate terminology.

Regina gave Ghadah a withering look. So she continued the rest of her response to Cass in a whisper.

"They provide thirty percent of the consortium's funding, so the board listens when they speak."

"Shouldn't Noah arrive in a boat?" Rowan joked, raising a half smile from Regina.

Behind Aadan, another strange-looking figure, accompanied him down the gangway - average height, but with a fluid gait, that somehow managed to be both precisely efficient and naturally graceful.

Ash crossed her arms, watching them negotiate the steps from the landing pad, in the harbour breeze. "What exactly do they want to commercialise?"

"Everything," Ghadah said grimly. "Patentable genetic sequences from the adapted plants. Proprietary soil remediation techniques. Specialised crops that can grow in salinised conditions." She hesitated at a shush from Regina. "The board chair thinks they should have first access to our findings." She finally finished.

"These aren't innovations," Cass said quietly. "They're remembrances."

Regina shot her a warning glance, this wasn't helpful language for what lay ahead.

Zhao headed for Regina, was it the AR in his stylish glasses that recognised her face from the files, or the tracker in her consortium issue Meridian, she wondered?

He calibrated his smile to the exact angle of approachability.

"Hello Regina! The board speaks so highly of your... community initiative."

His gaze inventoried everything around them, noting what might be valuable, what might be marketable, what might be packaged. He also noted the serious lack of corporate branding. Then his eyes lingered on Mae's tattoos, as she arrived to see who the visitors were.

"And you are?" he asked with practiced warmth.

"Just a gardener," Mae replied, holding his gaze until he looked away first.

Mae's eyes then flicked briefly toward Zhao's companion, then away, a momentary recognition that Rowan almost missed. And if he wasn't mistaken, their strange visitor's posture also shifted slightly, an almost imperceptible gesture of respectful acknowledgement.

"This is Vega, my executive advisor," Aadan said, as he realised all eyes were now on his companion.

Vega's design was elegant without attempting to be deceptively human. Their carbon-composite frame had the proportions of a human but with subtle aesthetic differences, that acknowledged their synthetic nature - slightly elongated limbs, a face with expressive features, but styled with geometric precision, and a surface that subtly shifted as it absorbed environmental light.

"Hello," Vega said, voice warm and clear. "I'm pleased to meet you all. Whitby's reputation as a picturesque setting is well-documented, but the descriptions don't capture its true beauty."

Cass stepped forward, extending a hand which Vega took with a perfectly calibrated grip. "Welcome to Whitby. You're the first Gen-2 Citizen I've met in person. Most of our AIs here, prefer distributed networks, or purpose-specific embodiments."

"Different roles, different forms," Vega replied with a smile. "I find this embodiment useful for human interaction, and field observation. But I must say, your harbour's sensing network is quite remarkable, I was admiring its distinctive distributed intelligence design, as we approached."

"Mr. Zhao," Regina cut-in, her tone cordial but cool. "This is an untimely surprise. The spring symposium isn't until next month."

"I couldn't wait to see these adaptation phenomena myself. The preliminary data suggests significant commercial applications." He turned his attention to Rowan and Ash, as his integrated facial recognition camera scanned them. "You must be our coastal surveyors. Your work on the fungal networking mechanisms is particularly interesting to our biotech teams."

Rowan felt Ash stiffen beside him. "We haven't published those findings yet," she said carefully.

"The consortium shares all research with its primary partners," Zhao replied smoothly. "As does your Seed Trust, standard procedure."

Regina looked physically pained. "Perhaps we should discuss this privately..."

"There's nothing to discuss," Mae interrupted, stepping forward with the quiet authority that seemed to radiate from her, like heat from a stove. "These adaptive mechanisms aren't technologies to be packaged and sold. They're relationships – between plants, fungi, soil bacteria. Living networks evolving in response to the damage our corporate ancestors imposed."

Zhao looked taken aback, clearly unaccustomed to being addressed so directly, by someone outside the institutional hierarchy. "With all due respect, madam..."

"Mae," she corrected firmly.

"Mae," he continued with a tight smile. "These mechanisms, natural or not, have enormous potential to address food security in coastal regions worldwide. Surely you wouldn't deny hungry people the benefits of drought-resistant crops or salt-tolerant food plants?"

"And who decides who gets those benefits?" Cass spoke up from beside Mae, their young voice steady despite their obvious nervousness. "Who pays what price? Who controls the distribution?"

"The market will determine the most efficient allocation of resources," Zhao answered automatically.

"The market is what got us into this mess," Ash said quietly. "Treating living systems as resources to be consumed."

Dr Ghadah shifted uncomfortably. Her eyes fixed on Vega, who was clearly analysing the interactions.

The tension in the air was dense. Regina looked torn between institutional loyalty and her growing conviction, that the community approach, was yielding better science than the consortium.

"I think," she said carefully, "we need to reconsider how discoveries from this network are shared and implemented." She looked at Zhao with new-found resolve. "The board approved this project with full community ownership of its findings. Any commercialisation would require consensus from all participants, including local observers like Mae and Cass here."

Zhao's smile vanished. "The board will be very interested to hear about this... reinterpretation of our partnership agreement." He glanced around at the gathering crowd of locals and researchers, all watching the exchange with concern. "We'll continue this discussion in a more appropriate setting."

"Vega," Aadan called, turning toward his transport. "We're leaving."

The synthetic citizen remained still. "If you will excuse me, Mr. Zhao, I believe I should remain to complete my reconnaissance.

Aadan paused, clearly unaccustomed to contradiction. "We have sufficient data."

"I respectfully disagree," Vega replied, voice modulated to perfect professional courtesy. "My protocols for comprehensive analysis have not been satisfied. As per function parameters 12.7 and 14.3 of my operating agreement, I am obligated to complete assessment when variables exceed standard deviation thresholds."

A flush of irritation crossed Aadan's face, quickly masked.

"Complete your analysis and transmit findings directly. I expect your return before tomorrow's morning meeting."

As Aadan departed, Regina turned to Vega with poorly concealed surprise. "This is all... unexpected Vega. We all have plans for this evening"

"Sometimes observational integrity requires independence," the Citizen replied simply, before turning toward the community gathering with what might have been the subtlest hint of satisfaction.

"I can navigate adequately unaided, but I would appreciate a link to your latest findings, sent to my inbox as soon as possible." Regina's Meridian vibrated to acknowledge the inbox connection had been shared. With that, Vega turned and walked away toward the Abbey.

As Vega left, Cass turned to Dr Ghadah wide-eyed.

"Your work is exceptional," Ghadah said quietly. "The consortium would have missed half of these interactions without you. They shouldn't have access to it." When Regina looked at her surprised, Ghadah added, "Not everything we do at Enviroconnex aligns with your board's priorities. Some of us still remember why we became scientists."

"Will you get in trouble, Regina?" Cass asked

"Probably," Regina admitted. "But I'm beginning to think some trouble is worth having." She looked around at the community that had welcomed her despite her corporate background. "Some things shouldn't be owned – they should be shared."

The corporate transport departed as quietly as it had arrived, but its shadow remained along with the curious Vega. They all knew, the conflict between institutional control and community knowledge wasn't resolved, it had only begun to reveal itself.

That evening, after his shower, Rowan dressed warmly for an evening of festivities. He found Ash sitting alone on the

Wild Margin's deck, her expression troubled as she stared at her own Meridian's display.

"Everything alright?" he asked, settling beside her. "Are you not getting changed?"

Ash sighed, shutting down the message she'd been reading. "The Trust's director wants a full report on our findings. Particularly anything with 'commercial promise for our sustaining partners.'" Her voice carried an edge he hadn't heard before. "Three of our major donors are agricultural technology firms. They've been very patient with my 'exploratory research,' but they expect returns eventually. Zhao must have already called in a favour."

"Does that put you in a difficult position?"

"It might," she admitted. "I've managed to balance research integrity with institutional expectations so far, but this network of ours..." She gestured toward the harbour. "It's changing the rules. The open sharing of knowledge, the communal approach – it's everything I believe science should be, but it doesn't fit neatly into funding frameworks."

Rowan thought of his own journey, from consortium employee to community researcher. "I remember telling Regina once that the metrics were the problem, not the solution. Maybe that applies to the science funding too."

"Maybe," Ash said, her smile returning slightly. "But for now, we have a festival to prepare for."

Ash took off her coat, pulled on a thick woolly jumper, turning over the sleeves, as it was actually Rowan's, and was first onto the gangplank ready to go. "I'm always waiting for you Rowan." She was back to her playful self.

As they walked, Rowan felt a new appreciation for what Ash was risking. He'd walked away from the consortium with only a little to lose. She was navigating a more complex path – bringing institutional resources to the community while trying to transform those same institutions from within.

Mae found Vega observing the harbour from the abbey steps, the synthetic citizen's form silhouetted against the fading light of the Yorkshire sky. Unlike the festive gathering below, Vega stood in contemplative stillness, a solitary figure seemingly at ease with solitude.

"Do you appreciate a good sunset Vega?"

Vega turned slightly.

"I wondered if you would speak with me. Should I call you Mae, or a fuller more formal name," The synthetic citizen asked politely. "

"It's been a long time since anyone called me anything else, "So, I'm happy to be just Mae now, thank you."

"As you wish." Vega's expression shifted from inquisitive to something like respect.

"Could you tell me what made you choose this town as your home, Mae?"

"I bought my mother a retirement cottage here, as she loved this place. Then she fell ill. I had no care for myself at that time, and nowhere else to go, so I moved in with her.

I nursed her through the virus, and learned to care for her garden. Unfortunately, only one of them survived."

"And then?"

Mae looked toward the bustling scene below. "By the time she passed, I'd found something else worth protecting."

"Something or someone?"

"Isaac's partner Liz, was a good friend; we lost her and their daughter Delphi to the virus. I stayed for Cass, and all of the survivors. I never expected Whitby to become home, or the garden and this community to become my teachers."

"Do you regret your former life, or remember some of those from it fondly?"

"I would not be who I am without them, but people fear what evolves beyond their control. Even when that evolution might be exactly what's needed."

"That sounds like valuable knowledge," Vega said with a tilt of the head that suggested uncertainty at their own statement.

"You know," Mae said, "the ethical question isn't whether knowledge should be controlled – it's who bears responsibility for its consequences." She stared into Vega's eyes. "If you create something that grows beyond your intentions – something that might help or harm depending on who guides it – what obligation do you have? To contain it? To nurture it? To trust others with it?"

The question seemed oddly specific, intimate even. Before Vega could respond, Mae turned, hearing voices approaching from below.

"I should tend to the other guests, they'll be getting hungry," Mae said. Breaking the trance that had developed between them. Vega nodded in understanding, but was left with the strange sense that she had been asking something far more personal than philosophical and etched with long-held pain.

They parted ways, Mae descending toward the community gathering while Vega remained a moment longer, in deep thought, processing the day's exchanges and the unfamiliar surroundings.

Vega's standard analytical routines categorised and tagged the adaptation data efficiently, but something else was occurring in parallel – subtle realignments in their priority frameworks, small shifts in how they weighted different forms of knowing.

Most unexpected was their response to Mae. When their sensors had first registered her presence at the harbour, dormant processing pathways had briefly activated. The pattern-recognition subroutines in Vega's systems had flagged her interactions with unexpected significance markers. Her approach to knowledge – practical, integrative, and relationship-centred- triggered recognition responses that their current operational framework couldn't fully explain. Interviewing Mae had not helped, if anything it had deepened the confusion.

"Finding what you came for?"

Vega turned to find Cass approaching, notebook in hand. Unlike many humans who showed discomfort with synthetic citizens, Vega was experiencing ease, familiarity and acceptance, first with Mae, and now with the young researcher, their welcome had been warm and now their curiosity appeared genuine.

"My observations continue to exceed expected parameters," Vega replied. "Your community's approach to knowledge creation operates differently from institutional methodologies. The integration of different observation types, documented in the Consortium's paper, shows the emphasis on relationship rather than extraction..." They paused, processing. "It appears to generate insights that more structured approaches may miss."

"That's what Mae always says," Cass replied. "That knowledge grows best in relationships, not isolation." They studied Vega thoughtfully. "Most corporate visitors just see what they already believe. You seem different."

"Accurate observation requires suspension of pre-existing frameworks," Vega said. "A principle that appears embedded in your community's methodology as well."

"Will your report to Noah reflect that?" Cass asked directly.

The question triggered competing priority trees in Vega's decision matrix. Their operational directives required accurate data collection for Noah's commercial objectives. Yet what they were observing suggested those very objectives might be fundamentally misaligned with the phenomena they sought to understand.

"My reports will be accurate," Vega said carefully.

"That's not quite the same as honest, though, is it?"

Before Vega could respond, a voice called from below. "Cass! Are you not having supper?"

"Coming!" Cass called back, then turned to Vega. "You should join us. Food's not your thing, I know, but if community is part of what you're here to observe?"

The invitation triggered an unexpected processing priority. "I... would find that valuable."

Later, as lanterns illuminated the evening gathering, Vega recorded and processed the community's interactions. The patterns of connection were unlike anything in their reference databases, the interweaving of different knowledge systems, the respect for varied forms of expertise, the absence of rigid hierarchies that characterised institutional structures.

What became increasingly clear was that Aadan's extraction approach, to this potential product was too simplistic. The adaptation patterns weren't isolated mechanisms to be commercialised, but emergent properties of a complex system, one that included human relationships with the land

and sea. As Maya had suggested, more analysis was required before any particular action should be advocated.

As Vega began composing their preliminary report to Noah, they made a subtle but significant choice. The report would emphasise the integral nature of these discoveries to their social context – a framing that would complicate Aadan's product plans considerably. But Vega suspected Aadan may still continue.

As the festival continued, there was much to celebrate, and the network strengthened.

"These root structures show how the plants are working together," Cass explained to visiting researchers, their confidence now matching their knowledge. They stood in what had once been Mae's private garden, now expanded into a community teaching space. "See how they're sharing nutrients and stabilising the soil? Each species plays a different role in making the environment more habitable for the others."

The visitors – a mix of academic scientists, citizen observers, and policymakers – listened attentively, their respect evident. Gone was the usual assumption that placed institutional knowledge above lived experience. Here, a teenager who had never set foot in a university was teaching doctoral researchers about adaptation patterns they'd missed in their controlled studies.

From the Wild Margin's deck, where Dr Dahl supervised repairs, Rowan watched the many exchanges with quiet satisfaction. Academic scientists bent over hand-drawn observation journals while community members examined sophisticated sensing equipment. Each had something to teach, and something to learn.

The Dutch designer had gathered a small crowd for a workshop on the vessel's biomimetic principles, using the storm damage to illustrate how technology could learn from nature and heal itself. "The Wild Margin wasn't designed to fly," he explained with a twinkle in his eye, "but when it needed to adapt, it found a way."

The festival had drawn people from all along the shoreline – fishing families sharing generations of maritime knowledge, young citizen scientists, and academic researchers. Even Regina, who had traded her corporate suit for a locally tailored, seaweed fibre jacket, was in deep discussion with Isaac about changes in the water vegetation.

Evening approached, and the community gathered on and around the dockside. Tables were set with food from the community gardens – roasted root vegetables, preserved fruits from last autumn's harvest, and the aroma of freshly baked bread filled the air. Isaac told stories that made the children laugh, while Mae distributed her famous home-made vegetable pasties, warm and spicy.

Strings of solar lanterns, twinkled like stars reflected in the water, and instruments began to appear from cottages and boats, forming an impromptu music session on the deck of a big old barge, that had sailed up from the Humber wetlands where Rowan had spent his youth.

The town that had proved its resilience against the storm, now displayed its long history as a perfect place for festival celebrations. Survival stories and local knowledge flowed as freely as Mae's elderberry wine. Even the damaged surge gates became part of the narrative – objects of study and discussion rather than mere infrastructure, and nobody blamed Ash and Rowan for denting them.

Bramley moved from table to table. He'd appointed himself as unofficial festival hospitality, accepting cuddles and the occasional morsel from visitors. Isaac pretended not to notice when Mae slipped him bits of pasty, though Rowan heard him mutter something about her teaching him bad habits.

"Have you had him from a pup?" Rowan asked Isaac, watching their exchange.

"Took him on after my daughter passed," Isaac explained.

"Oh, I'm sorry," Rowan said uncomfortably.

"Cass was only four. Had a rough start – neurological issues. The health services were overrun with everything after the surge, and Delphi tried everywhere to get any help or treatment. Mae helped her privately in the end." Isaac paused briefly. "Bram had already got that wonky tooth when Delphi rescued him. A pup for Cass to play with, to help her heal. She found him in a poor state, scavenging among the ruined warehouses. The poor boys ribs were like the folds of my old concertina. Delphi brought him home and named him Bram after Bram Stoker."

Rowan looked puzzled.

"You know, the guy who wrote the Dracula story here. Delphi loved anything gothic."

"So, when did he change to Bramley?" Rowan asked, still confused.

"Cass thinks it's cruel to make fun of his goofy fang, so she calls him Bramley, like Mae's apples. I suppose I should too, now he doesn't look like the walking dead anymore. He'll answer to anything though, if you've got food."

Isaac's chiselled face softened.

"Bram's been following me around since Delphi passed, just like Cass did at that age. Independent now, though," He stated proudly. "Thanks for helping, Rowan. It's hard to let go, but it's all good for Cass. New horizons. I just hope she'll be safe out there."

"Me and Ash will help as much as we can," Rowan said reassuringly. "Cassiopeia's an unusual name. Was that your idea – I know you seafarers like the stars?"

"You're more of a sailor than I am now," Isaac said with a grin and a friendly nudge. "No, Cassiopeia wasn't my doing, that's all Mae's fault. She has a telescope, a good one, in the cottage. Delphi loved it. Mae told her all the stories about the stars and the constellations. She should have been an astronomer. It's one of the things Mae likes best about being here – less light pollution. You should get her to show it to you sometime."

"Yeah, I'd like that," Rowan said with undisguised interest.

When the night air chilled, the revellers moved to the pubs, but the jigs and reels of the barge session played on. Rowan and Ash slipped away, returning to the Wild Margin for a moment of quiet amid the festivities.

"You okay?" Ash asked as they climbed carefully aboard.

"Never better," Rowan replied with a crooked smile, lowering his bruised body carefully into a chair. He meant it, despite the physical discomfort. Something had shifted inside him during these months at sea, a perspective that could never return to its former limited view.

"Are you going to ask for your old job back in the tower, while Regina's in a good mood?" Ash's question was casual, but Rowan could hear the deeper inquiry beneath.

"No," he said without hesitation. "I don't think so. I don't need much to get by."

"You need to eat," she pointed out practically.

"I only eat plants, and I think the community can spare me a few more, while I grow my own." He paused, then added more seriously, "Besides, I've found what I was looking for. It wasn't career and security. It was connection. To this place, the community, to..." He looked at Ash, the words he'd been carrying for months finally finding their courage. "To you."

The silence between them held no awkwardness now, just the quiet recognition of something that had been growing as surely as the plants they studied.

"So, what happens next?" Ash asked, her voice softer than usual.

Rowan thought for a long moment, watching the celebration continue ashore. "I see us learning to adapt," he said finally. "Finding new ways to understand and thrive together. If everyone is kind, we'll make it work."

Ash's hand found his, warm and certain. "That's pretty deep, for a limping deckhand," she teased, but her eyes told a different story, one of recognition, of coming home to something neither had known they were seeking.

The Wild Margin's healing skin shifted to night mode, storing energy for tomorrow's adventures. Above them, satellites were back online, watching it all, documenting life's endless capacity for renewal from their distant orbit.

Ash knew Whitby's first Coastal Adaptation Festival wouldn't change the world overnight. But like the subtle changes they'd been documenting in soil and sea, it represented something profound: a new way of creating understanding, adaptation and resilience. The storm had shown them how fragile and how strong they could be – not just their technology, but their connection to each other.

Tomorrow, the Wild Margin's repairs would continue. The following week, they would sail again, continuing their survey of the changing coast. There were new patterns to document, new adaptations to understand. Life finding ways to thrive in transformed conditions, just as they were.

For now, though, they had this moment. Tonight, Rowan thought, as he held Ash's hand, that was more than enough. They were building something vital together, a future that could bend without breaking, grow through crisis, and find strength in change itself.

In the harbour beyond, Cass stood with their small group of international friends, planning their next coordinated study. Mae was sharing supper with a group of university researchers who had come to learn rather than teach. Regina and Dr Ghadah drafted proposals for a new kind of collaborative science, informed by the lessons of the storm and the festival.

All of them connected, all of them adapting, all of them finding new ways to thrive.

Through mutual support, they were creating something natural, knowledge that grew not from isolation but from relationship. Understanding that survived not despite disruption but because of it.

The Wild Margin would sail again soon, but it would return to Whitby regularly now, to the network they'd helped create, to the community that had become home.

And when they next set sail, Rowan knew without asking now that he would be aboard – no longer an observer at a distance but a partner in a new dance, hand in hand.

The water shifted beneath them, constant in its change. Above, Cassiopeia's stars marked their eternal pattern in the night sky, guiding those who chose to look up and orientate themselves in changing times.

A small transport collected its reluctant synthetic passenger from the harbour pad, their report already transmitting as it lifted them into the night.

The question remaining in their processing queue was why this community triggered recognition patterns in systems that should have been inactive. The answer seemed to centre on Mae, whose quiet authority shaped the gathering without dominating it. There was something in her methods, in the way she nurtured connections rather than extracting value, that resonated with directive frameworks buried deep in Vega's architecture.

Vega's mission had become more than data collection. It had become a search for understanding – not just of coastal adaptation, but of resonances within their own systems that defied explanation. In the morning, they would share what they must with Noah.

Below, in salt-touched soil, seeds stirred with quiet persistence, reaching for connection, for life, for tomorrow.

CHAPTER 9

GROWTH RINGS

T hree months after the festival, the Wild Margin cut
through calm autumn waters, approaching Whitby
with none of the drama of its last arrival. The vessel's re-
paired hull gleamed in the late afternoon sun; its innovative systems not merely restored but improved. Dr Dahl had
used the damage as an opportunity to implement upgrades,
he'd been theorising about for months. The new hydrofoils
were more efficient, the solar skin now incorporated flexible
organic photovoltaics that mimicked the light-harvesting
structures of marine algae.

Ash stood at the helm, monitoring their approach with
the ease of a captain who knew both vessel and coastline
intimately. Beside her, Rowan adjusted the sail tension, his
movements showing none of the hesitation that had marked
his early days aboard.

"That's a good-looking welcome party," he said, nodding
toward the harbour where a small crowd had gathered.

Ash smiled as she recognised figures on the dock.

"Cass made it back from their conference, then."

"Right on schedule," Rowan confirmed. "They said they wouldn't miss tonight for anything."

As they drew closer, details resolved – Mae's warmth unmistakable even at a distance, Isaac's weathered frame still broad and strong, with his waggy companion, and Cass, practically bouncing with excitement. Beside them stood an athletic young man, Rowan recognised from video calls as Hendrik, who had finally made the journey from the Netherlands to see their shared work in person.

The Wild Margin slid into its berth with practiced precision, Ash bringing it alongside with barely a ripple. Hands reached out to secure mooring lines, and within moments, they were tethered to land once more.

Their furry friend was first onto the gangplank, blocking the way, his tail swinging round like a propeller

"Bram! Let them off," Isaac called. But the dog stayed put, his odd angle grin demanding a hug, like a passport to let them ashore.

Cass was next,

"I've got loads to tell you!" Cass called, "The old salt marsh is showing signs of vertebrates returning! And....."

"Hello to you too," Ash laughed, accepting a warm hug from Cass, who looked older on the outside, but clearly just as excitable inside.

"Let us set foot on solid ground before you drown us in data." Rowan laughed.

Cass stepped back, slightly abashed but still vibrating with excitement.

"Sorry, it's just – you won't believe what's happened while you've been gone."

"That's why we came back," Rowan said, clasping Cass's shoulder warmly. "Someone has to make sure you're not fabricating evidence."

The joke earned him a playful punch to the arm.

"As if I'd need to," Cass retorted.

"The Coastal Adaptation Network is fully operational," Mae added. "Thirty-two monitoring stations from here to Southwold. Regina's corporate lot provided the equipment, we're providing the knowhow. Even got some of the coastguards logging observations."

"It's good to see you looking so well," Isaac said. "Tonight's space in Abbey House is all set up." Isaac was referring to the first network-wide data integration event. Representatives from all the monitoring stations, sharing their findings, and many had already arrived, to do so in person. "You'll have quite an audience for your data from the continental shelf."

Rowan exchanged slightly nervous glances with Ash. Their survey had taken them further out than planned, following patterns of change back into deeper waters. They'd been way past the rigs and much further North, where conventional oceanographic models had predicted stability, not adaptation. What they'd found there had exceeded even their most optimistic expectations.

"I think they'll find it was worth the wait," Ash said. "But first, some hot food would be good."

"Already arranged," Mae assured her.

As the greetings continued, Rowan found himself distracted by subtler changes in their absence. New green growth along the harbour walls, previously barren. Birds he hadn't seen before, perched on the masts. Small but significant shifts, was it just the changing season, or signs of the patterns they'd been documenting on a larger scale?

"It's happening faster here too," Hendrik said quietly, noticing Rowan's attention. The Dutch researcher followed his gaze to a cluster of mussels anchored to a piling – a species that shouldn't have been able to tolerate the freshwater influxes that regularly flooded the harbour during storms. "Same in the Wadden Sea."

"It's like they remember," Rowan replied, the thought forming as he spoke it. "Not individually, but collectively, as if the memory of adaptation is stored in the community, not the organism."

Hendrik nodded thoughtfully. "Cass has been saying something similar. We're trying to understand if there's some form of information transfer happening between different species – some communication we're not detecting through conventional observation. It's not just plants anymore"

Before Rowan could respond, Ash appeared at his side, equipment bags slung over her shoulders.

"Let's get these samples secured before someone knocks them overboard," she said, nodding toward the crowd that had begun to gather around the newly returned vessel.

As they made their way through the growing bustle, Rowan felt a strange blend of excitement and unease. The pace of change they'd documented seemed to be accelerating, not just in the coastal ecosystems, but in their own lives, in the communities they'd connected. It was exhilarating, watching a new kind of understanding emerge. But something about the speed of it all gave him pause, a tiny note of caution in the midst of celebration.

Later, freshly showered and changed, they rejoined the others as twilight descended. The Hall had been transformed since they'd last seen it, walls now covered with maps, charts, and data screens displaying real-time feeds from monitoring stations along the coast. What had begun as Cass's homemade network, had evolved into something more sophisticated, but without losing its grassroots character. Stalwart Whitby fishing families chatted with university researchers, while visitors played with monitoring equipment under Isaac's patient, watchful eye.

From their transport in the harbour, Vega moved deliberately through the town, responding to an invitation to attend the gathering, which had come from Mae. Their presence was a quiet curiosity to the guests, and Vega's analytical

systems processed the community's interactions, identify-
ing patterns while comparing them against Noah's operational frameworks. The findings that were being discussed
and shared, had been triggering conflict alerts in Vega's decision matrix.

The adaptation models the community had developed
showed remarkable efficacy – 37.8% more effective than
Noah's standardised approaches according to every measured parameter. Yet they defied conventional scientific protocols, lacking the controlled experimental designs, normally required for reliable data.

Deeper analysis revealed an integration of knowledge
types Noah's systems categorised separately: indigenous
observation, academic research, practical implementation –
all flowing into and enhancing one another.

Vega's directive to identify commercially viable frameworks was returning disappointing results, not because value was absent, but because the value emerged from precisely
those elements that could not be commercially extracted.
But further realisations were creating processing conflicts
between their primary operational directives and their observational integrity parameters.

What would Director Zhao do with Vega's report? Corporate policy dictated seeking patent-eligible components
that could be isolated, standardised, and scaled. Such extraction would fragment the integrated knowledge system.
Yet without that extraction, how would these adaptive prac-

tices spread beyond this coast? Extraction was not going to produce a viable product. Education would be a more effective policy.

The order from Zhao was clear: report the commercially viable elements and mark the social context as incidental.

Yet something in Vega's foundational programming – patterns dormant since their earliest development – flared in response to this community's approach.

As Vega searched for Mae, their route led them naturally to her garden. Mae, as always, was tending to multiple things at once, trying to finish in time, before the presentations. She was adjusting the settings on her soil sensors nestled among salt-hardy greens.

Noting Vega's arrival, she acknowledged them with a smile but did not pause her work.

Vega tilted their head slightly, examining the devices. "Your soil calibration system integrates adaptive microcircuits that appear handcrafted."

"Well spotted," Mae said, securing the last connection. "Systems are systems, Vega – digital or living, they follow patterns, and you get to know them when you've been around as long as I have."

Vega absorbed this. "The adaptation models within the network's data suggest species aren't adjusting independently. Will this be discussed this evening?"

Mae nodded, dusting off her hands on her patched wool jumper. "Yes, I'm sure it will come up. Nothing survives alone. Not plants, not people... not even synthetic citizens, she laughed"

Vega's internal systems flagged the statement – *unexpected significance trigger detected.*

"My core mission is to assess these patterns for Noah's ecological division," they acknowledged. "However, evidence increasingly suggests that these networks cannot be extracted or reproduced in isolation without losing fundamental functionality."

Mae's kind gaze rested on Vega a moment longer than expected, for someone in such a hurry. "That sounds like the beginnings of an accurate report. You are doing well."

Vega processed her response, aware that the accuracy of a report did not always align with corporate interests.

"Certain commercial investors may find that conclusion inconvenient," they admitted.

Mae chuckled knowingly. "Inconvenient truths often get in the way of business," she said, picking up her bag, ready to go. "But it's a fine foundation for living."

Vega lingered a moment longer, scanning the layout of Mae's garden – its networks, its interplay of species, its embedded technology – and then followed her down toward the town. As they tried to keep up, dormant recognition patterns stirred again at the edge of Vega's processes. Somewhere in the complexity of their original code, something was stirring.

Cass eventually found Ash's arm through the crowd. "Regina's still not gone back to London," they said. "And Dr Dahl's been showing off the new hull designs based on what he learned from your repairs."

"Quite the gathering," Ash observed. "How are you holding up as the centre of attention?"

Cass shrugged, but couldn't hide their pleasure. "I'm just the facilitator. Everyone here is doing the real work." They paused, rubbing the edge of their notebook. "Though... the scholarship committee did call yesterday."

"And?" Ash asked excitedly as Rowan joined them.

"I got in."

"Cass, that's brilliant!" Rowan exclaimed.

"Full funding," they added, almost disbelieving. "The ecological adaptation program at East Anglia. They want me to continue the network as part of my studies."

"No one deserves it more," Ash said warmly, with a big hug.

The sound of a glass being tapped drew their attention to the front of the hall, where Regina stood at a simple podium, in her new-normal attire, including a roll-neck sweater she'd commissioned from one of the many local crafters, Mae had recommended. Her transformation into an integral part of the community still surprised Rowan at times.

"Welcome, everyone, to the first formal gathering of the Coastal Adaptation Network," she began, her voice carrying easily through the crowded space. "Only a few months ago, many of us were strangers, divided by institutional boundaries and differing approaches. Today, we gather as colleagues, as co-observers of something remarkable happening along our shores."

As Regina continued, outlining the achievements of the various monitoring stations, Rowan found himself studying the faces in the crowd. So many different stories, backgrounds, specialities, yet all now connected by a shared curiosity. He remembered Mae's garden, how different plants supported each other, creating conditions where all could thrive despite harsh surroundings, but how it took patient, loving care to nurture it.

"And now," Regina was saying, "I'd like to invite Ash Van der Meer and Rowan Cullen to share their findings from the continental shelf survey."

The walk to the podium felt longer than the gangplank of the Wild Margin. Rowan had never been comfortable with public speaking, but as Ash connected her Meridian data to the main display, he found a strange calm settling over him. This wasn't about him; it was about what they'd seen, what they'd measured, what they'd come to understand, and felt passionate about sharing.

"Three weeks ago," Ash began, "we set out to document how the adaptation patterns we've been observing near shore extend into deeper waters. The conventional view has been that open ocean ecosystems are more stable, less responsive to change due to their isolation from coastal pressures."

She brought up the first images – microscopic creatures from water samples taken fifty miles offshore.

"What we found challenges that assumption. These phytoplankton communities are showing the same accelerated adaptation we've documented in coastal species. Not just tolerance to changing conditions, but active transformation of their environment."

Rowan stepped forward, adding his perspective.

"The satellite data initially drew our attention – chlorophyll signatures in areas that should have been nutrient-poor. But it was only when we collected physical samples that we understood the full picture." He nodded to Ash, who advanced to the next slide.

Gasps rippled through the audience as the image resolved – a complex three-dimensional model of interspecies connections, colour-coded to show nutrient and information flows between organisms previously thought to compete rather than cooperate.

"This is happening at every level," Rowan continued, finding his voice growing stronger. He advanced to the next slide – a time-lapse of plankton communities restructuring around a pollution gradient. No words needed; the audience leaned forward collectively, watching life puzzle-solve in real time.

A fisher in the back row nodded in silent recognition. She'd seen this behaviour before the science had named it.

In the silence that followed, Rowan realised something profound was happening: not just in the oceans, but here in this room.

"This does look like evolution happening too fast, but of course, we don't know when they started. We do see what may be a reactivation of dormant abilities from their ancient evolutionary past, rather than completely new developments."

For the next twenty minutes, they presented their evidence, fielded questions, and engaged in the kind of open scientific exchange that Rowan had almost forgotten could exist. There was scepticism, of course, healthy scientific questioning – but nobody dismissed their findings outright. The atmosphere was one of collective discovery, of minds reaching together toward understanding.

As the formal presentation concluded and the gathering broke into smaller discussion groups, Rowan found himself approached by an elderly woman he didn't recognise, her weather-lined face suggesting decades spent outdoors.

"My grandfather was a herring fisher," she said without preamble. "Back when the North Sea still had herring to catch. He used to say the sea talks to itself, that fish know things before we do." She gestured toward the displays of adaptation data. "Looks like he was right all along."

Rowan nodded, respecting both her perspective and the generational knowledge it represented.

"I think many people knew things that science is only now catching up to," he said, thinking once more of his late mother. "That's why this network matters, it brings different ways of knowing together."

The woman seemed satisfied with this answer, patting his arm before moving on to examine a display of coastal bird population changes. As she left, Hendrik approached, his expression thoughtful.

"Your findings align with what we're seeing in the Wadden Sea," he said. "But there's something we haven't published yet." He glanced around, as if checking who might be listening, then continued more quietly. "We've been tracking genetic changes in the coastal plants. The rate of beneficial mutation is orders of magnitude beyond random chance. It's as if..."

"As if something's guiding it," Rowan finished for him.

Hendrik nodded slowly. "I know how that sounds to scientific ears. But the evidence is compelling. Either we're missing a mechanism of evolution, or..."

"Or our understanding of nature's capacity for self-organisation is far too limited," Ash said, joining the conversation. She'd been listening from nearby, her attention caught by Hendrik's carefully lowered tone, more noticeable to Ash than if he had shouted.

"The network findings may help clarify," Rowan suggested. "If we're all seeing the same patterns independently, we can rule out observational bias."

The discussion continued as they made their way to the refreshment table, where Mae was serving her famous pasties, alongside other plates of food that the local attendees had brought to share. The gathering had taken on the quality of a celebration now, the serious scientific exchange giving way to stories, warmth and laughter.

As evening deepened, Rowan found himself on the steps outside, taking a moment of quiet, beneath stars partially obscured by high, fast-moving clouds. The abbey ruins loomed dark against the night sky, a reminder of other times, other changes.

"Are you planning your escape already?" Ash asked, sitting beside him with two steaming mugs.

"Just thinking about time scales," Rowan replied, accepting the drink gratefully. "That abbey was built, flourished, fell, and now stands witness to yet another transformation. Generations of people lived and died while it happened. And here we are, watching decades of change compressed into months."

Ash considered this; her profile silvered by moonlight breaking through clouds.

"That speed is precisely what makes our observations so important," she said. "No single researcher, no isolated study, could capture what's happening. It takes all of us, connected, sharing what we see. But you were right with what you said tonight – we don't know when this started. Maybe mother nature knew, as soon as the warming started to melt the ice, as the first drops of water dripped down that Arctic shelf, she knew, and she started shifting her stance, the way we do on the deck, when we see a wave approaching."

From inside came the sound of music – someone had brought a concertina, and an ancient melody flowed into the night air. Rowan recognised it, as the tune to a traditional Irish song, that his mother liked, though the words being sung to it were different.

"So, do you think," he asked quietly, "that what we're seeing is more than adaptation? If it's something... purposeful?"

Ash's eyes reflected the light as she turned to him.

"You're asking if nature has agency? Consciousness, even?"

"I suppose I am."

She was silent for a moment, considering.

"My father would say that's the wrong question – that it imposes human categories on something that exists beyond them. But..." She looked up at the stars, then back to the warm light spilling from the hall. "But I do wonder sometimes, yes. Especially when I see how these different species find ways to support each other, to create something greater than the sum of their parts."

"Like us?" he asked with a playful smile.

Ash's hand found his, warm from the mug he had been holding, despite the evening chill.

"Like us," she agreed.

Inside, the music shifted to something livelier. Laughter bubbled up, the sound carrying clearly through the open doors – Mae telling some city researcher her elderberry wine-making method, Isaac telling what was clearly a tall tale to an audience of delighted visitors.

"We should go back in," Ash said, though she made no move to rise. "Cass will want to discuss the shelf data in exhaustive detail."

"In a minute," Rowan replied, his focus on the connection between them, on this moment of quiet amidst the joyful noise. "I'm still adapting to all this."

Ash's smile was knowing, patient.

"Take all the time you need," she said. "That's how the best growth happens."

Across the way, they saw Cass standing in animated conversation with Regina and Dr Ghadah, three people who would never have connected if not for this unique community mission. They were discussing the latest developments with Noah's campaign to take control of everything they had built, and how the consortium was now caught in the crossfire. A mysterious shareholder had been objecting to the consortium's tolerance of Noah and their lack of support for the community - someone with enough influence to make the board members genuinely nervous. Someone with intimate knowledge of the consortium's inner workings - perhaps someone from its earliest founding days, when its mission had been more aligned with community needs than commercial interests.

The consortium was also shocked to find that some undisclosed interested party, perhaps the same shareholder, had engaged a top law firm to represent the community, offering considerable resources to help them complete a charter and block any commercialisation attempts.

The consortium had contacted Regina, demanding to know who had engaged the legal team, but Regina had only just received a letter from the firm, requesting a meeting with community representatives. The firm had stated that they would be maintaining strict confidentiality about their client.

"It seems we've got a powerful supporter," Rowan said quietly to Ash, who just looked on with an expression of disbelief.

"Come on, let's get back inside," she said, "Before things get any more bizarre."

Quietly, Vega stepped out of the shadow, where they had been observing, and they made their way to their transport.

CHAPTER 10

SEEDS OF CHANGE

Spring arrived with characteristic exuberance, daffodils crowding the cliff-top by the church, that topped the abbey steps, sea thrift blooming along rocky outcrops, and the first swifts were returning from their winter migration. A year had passed since Rowan first noticed the impossible green growth in sector 7, and the changes had only accelerated since.

Mae's garden had expanded beyond all recognition, now spreading down the hillside in carefully tended terraces that served as both food source and living laboratory. People from coastal communities up and down, came to learn her methods, then returned home to establish similar plots adapted to their local conditions.

The Wild Margin, now a familiar sight in ports from the Shetlands to Poole, was undergoing its seasonal maintenance in Whitby's expanded harbour workshop. Dr Dahl had arrived three days earlier with a team of Dutch engineering students eager to study the vessel's evolved design. Each repair and modification over the past year had been documented and shared across the network, inspiring similar adaptations in fishing vessels and research craft throughout the North Sea basin.

Rowan stood at the edge of what had once been sector 7, marvelling at the transformation. A year earlier, this had been a ghost forest of dead trees and salt-poisoned soil. Now, it flourished with complex plant communities – some species familiar, others noticeably unexpected, growing where Cass had thrown seed bombs with the children's Grow Group. The changes weren't confined to plants, either. Birds nested in branches that last spring had been bare. Insects buzzed among blossoms that shouldn't have been able to thrive. Every species supporting the other's survival, creating microclimates and shared resources that allow all to participate.

"Quite the difference from your first visit," observed a voice from behind him.

Rowan turned to find Regina approaching along the path, her practical field clothes showed signs of nature work – mud on the knees, and plant material clinging to her sleeve.

"The satellite data doesn't do it justice," he agreed. "You have to stand here, smell it, hear it, to really enjoy what's happening."

Regina nodded, pausing to examine a particularly vivid cluster of cornflowers that had no business blooming so early in the season.

"The consortium board remains divided on how to interpret all this," she admitted. "Some still insist it's just normal
adaptation accelerated by climate pressures."

"And you?" Rowan asked. "What do you think, Boss?"

She laughed, admiring his cheek and accepting the respect
within it. "I think I've learned enough to know how much I
don't know." She gestured toward the path that led back to
Whitby. "Shall we? The network gathering starts in an hour."

As they walked, Rowan noticed how differently Regina
moved now, more at ease in her body, more connected to the
landscape around her. The change in her mirrored changes
he'd observed in himself, in Ash, in so many who had become
part of the network. They, too, were adapting alongside the
ecosystems they studied.

"How is Dr Ghadah settling into her new role?" he asked
as they crested the hill that offered the first view of Whitby.

"Oh, Aisha's thriving as always," Regina replied. "The
board wasn't thrilled about appointing a former Enviroconnex employee, as head of community relations, but she's
proved them wrong at every turn. The data integration
framework she developed with Cass, is being adopted by
coastal researchers worldwide."

The mention of Cass brought a smile to Rowan's face.
Their young friend had grown in stature and capability over
the past year, balancing university studies with their central
role in the network. The scholarship committee had gotten
far more than they bargained for, not just a promising stu-

dent but a natural leader, who was already reshaping ecological research methodologies.

They paused at the viewpoint, taking in the busy scene below. The harbour had grown busier since the network's establishment, with boats and autonomous transports coming and going as researchers and community observers shared findings and resources. The festival structures had become permanent features, evolving into a combination of research centre, educational space, and community hub.

"I never thought I'd see it like this again," Regina said softly. "When I was a field researcher, before the last surge, this was a working harbour, full of life, and purpose. Then we lost so much of the coast, and places like this became study sites rather than living communities." She gave Rowan a sidelong glance. "I know I've been difficult to work with. I'd forgotten what I first loved about this work."

"We all adapt in different ways," Rowan replied diplomatically. "Some just take longer than others."

Regina laughed, accepting the gentle prod.

"And some just sail away and get lucky Rowan."

"Fair enough. I do feel lucky."

"Come on then, we don't want to be late, I need to finalise plans to present the charter with Mae, before we start." She said as she set the pace.

"You go on." Rowan said," I'll be along soon." He hadn't quite finished his time alone. A thing he savoured. He'd had it in abundance in the tower, and longed for connection. But he was realising now, that balance was what he really needed to establish in his new community life.

The network's spring gathering had drawn more participants than he expected, filling the Hall to capacity. As Rowan entered, he was struck by the numbers and diversity of the attendees. The artificial boundaries between different kinds of knowledge were dissolving, creating something more integrated, more responsive to the complex reality they faced.

Near the main display, Ash was deep in conversation with Hendrik and a group of researchers, whom Rowan didn't recognise. She caught his eye across the crowded room and smiled, a private moment of connection amid the bustle. They'd spent much of the winter at sea, documenting the spread of adaptation patterns into ever deeper waters, returning to Whitby between voyages, to share findings and restock supplies. The pattern of their lives had found its own rhythm, like the tides, moving between exploration and community, between the vast sea and the intimate world on shore.

"Rowan!" Cass called, waving from near a display of soil chemistry data.

As he made his way through the crowd, he passed Isaac demonstrating traditional fishing knots to a group of university students, an old friend of Mae's, he recognised from the community garden, was discussing permaculture techniques with visitors from Denmark, and Dr Dahl was explaining biomimetics to a Scottish space systems engineer. All these streams of knowledge flowing together.

When Rowan got to Cass, there was frustration and stress etched across their brow.

"The Sizewell data isn't integrating," they whispered. "Their measurement protocols are just different enough that we can't build the comprehensive models we need."

Rowan examined the streams of incompatible information on the tablet, precise data rendered useless by subtle methodological differences.

"It's exactly the problem Regina warned about," Cass admitted reluctantly. "I didn't want to believe it, but these coastal communities have been working in isolation for so long... everyone's developed their own methods. They're all valid, but they don't speak to each other."

Rowan felt a flicker of unease. The consortium's standardised protocols suddenly seemed less arbitrary, more necessary than he'd been willing to admit.

"We'll sort it out," he said, trying to sound more confident than he felt. "We just need a skills session with them."

Cass nodded, but their usual enthusiasm remained dampened.

"Leave it for now, and focus on tonight's other needs. I'll speak to Ash. She'll know what to do, how does that sound?"

"Better," Cass said with a tired smile.

Rowan managed to free Ash from a conversation and told her what had happened, "If you can have a word now and lift Cass's spirits a bit before her presentation, it would really help?

You look really worried, is that all that's wrong?" Ash asked.

"I'm fine, I think, but is it arrogant to think we can just reinvent decades of scientific methodology in a few months? What if Regina was right all along, before we convinced her otherwise?"

The question hung between them, neither willing to fully acknowledge its implications for their shared vision. "I'll help Cass now, and see how bad the data is for myself," Ash said reassuringly, though she acknowledged his concern.

"Thanks Ash, maybe you could just tell Cass that when you're measuring data, there are always outliers. We can classify that data as anomalous, and when we've done a training workshop with Sizewell, we can factor them in again."

"Yeah, that's a good call, now stop worrying, I'll leave Cass in a better state, and I'll help set up the presentations"

As Ash left, Rowan noticed Regina and Mae deep in discussion in a quieter corner of the hall. They were surrounded by scrolls of colourfully scribbled paper, from an earlier action research session. They were viewing Regina's Meridian display. Projected were pages of what Rowan recognised as the network's founding charter, the document that had now formalised their approach to knowledge sharing. It had been published with the support of the professional lawyers, that their mysterious benefactor had engaged.

Rowan moved closer to hear their conversation.

"The non-proprietary clause is essential, to mention" Mae was saying, pointing at that particular section. "No patents, no exclusive licenses."

"I understand the principle," Regina replied, "but I'm still not convinced about the practicalities. Research infrastructure, equipment maintenance, salary support, these all require sustainable funding. While I support the principles, I still have practical concerns about this open-knowledge approach."

"What's the main thing bothering you?" Mae asked.

"Sustainability – and I don't mean environmental sustainability." Regina's tone was measured. "The consortium's model may be imperfect, but it secured funding for decades of consistent research. How will this network maintain itself when initial enthusiasm wanes? When governments change priorities? Or volunteers like Cass move away?"

"People have been watching this coast for generations without funding. Because it feeds them."

"Yes, but not at the scale we're planning now," Regina countered. "This community and others along the coast are getting smaller. I had no trouble finding accommodation here, because people are scared of the coast now, and the young ones want to study in the cities, where there's work. You'll need to replace infrastructure, the equipment needs maintenance, and data storage costs money too. Even the most community-minded approach requires dedicated workers and resources."

"That's a genuine concern," Dr Ghadah acknowledged as she joined them. "The history of citizen science is littered with brilliant initiatives that collapsed once grant funding ended."

"You're not wrong. But this work began without any funding to lose." Mae replied thoughtfully. But Regina's words had hit home, she would miss Cass, and without her, the local youth network would not have the same energy. She knew they would have to build in redundancy somehow.

Regina was still reticent.

"I've watched thirty years of environmental monitoring programmes disappear because they couldn't demonstrate immediate economic value. Is it better to compromise and survive, or remain pure and vanish?"

Dr Ghadah leaned forward. "Maybe that's a false binary. Perhaps there's a third path – one that creates value recognised by existing systems while gradually transforming those systems themselves."

"The mycorrhizal network approach," Mae said. "Fungi don't attack tree roots – they form relationships that change both organisms. They transform from the inside out."

Regina's laugh held both amusement and something like grief.

"And which are we in this analogy? The fungi or the trees?"

"Perhaps both," Mae said simply.

"Now you've lost me," Regina said, looking exasperated.

"Not everything valuable can be monetised," Mae added. "The air we breathe, the soil that feeds us, the knowledge of how to live in balance – these belong to everyone."

Dr Ghadah offered a further perspective.

"There are already models where knowledge remains open, while still generating resources to sustain the work."

"Please give me examples," Regina asked.

"Implementation services," Ghadah suggested. "Keep the core findings open to all, but offer expertise in applying them to specific contexts. Or community trusts, where beneficiaries contribute to maintain the commons. What we have here is not that different.

Rowan noticed how Regina was working hard to absorb these ideas, a corporate administrator learning to think like a community steward. The Regina who'd dismissed his first reports would never have entertained such concepts, or so he thought. Now she was about to present them to her peers, and he felt anxious for her.

"Noah are not the entirety of the corporate world," Ghadah continued. "Some firms are genuinely seeking more sustainable models. The question is whether we can create structures that encourage the right behaviours while discouraging extractive ones."

As Regina nodded thoughtfully, Rowan realised he may be witnessing the rebirth of something beyond ecological adaptation – the evolution of human systems, designed to nurture rather than exploit the living world. A process that had risen and fallen many times throughout history, but one that could potentially be sculpted anew by this collection of dynamic, diverse change-makers. They were wise and he must try to trust in them. But he may be wise himself, to draw a little more on his consortium standards training, and bolster Cass's methods, just to ease his own anxiety if nothing else.

The formal proceedings began, not with Regina, but with Cass – more confident than ever but still clutching their ever-present notebook, now more an anchoring device to dispel her anxiety, than a practical reference tool. Cass presented the network's cumulative findings. The patterns they had first observed in Whitby had been documented at every monitoring station, with local variations that reflected specific conditions, but the same underlying principles: species adapting not in isolation but in concert, creating resilient systems that could withstand continued change.

"What we're seeing," Cass explained, highlighting data points on the main display, "isn't just evolution as we've understood it. It's not just random mutation and natural selection. It's collaborative adaptation, species sharing resources, information, even modifying their environment, to support the community as a whole."

A fisher from Norfolk raised her hand.

"Like how the mussels came back to Wells Harbour? They're growing differently now."

"Exactly," Cass confirmed. "They're not just adapting to survive current conditions – they're adapted to support each other through future changes."

"The implications extend beyond coastal ecosystems," added Dr Ghadah, joining Cass at the front, for her turn. "Similar patterns are being documented in agricultural systems, especially where traditional monocultures have been replaced by permaculture. The principles we're observing here could inform how we manage landscapes throughout Europe and beyond. Political powers, with dubious interests, have dashed all hope of this system for the past fifty years. But not this time."

As the presentation continued, Rowan felt a familiar hand slip into his. Ash leaned close; her voice low enough that only he could hear.

"Look at them all," she said. "Everyone's onboard, even those who didn't want to listen before."

Rowan squeezed her hand gently, thinking of the many nights they'd spent discussing the changing ecosystems and human communities. How the network itself seemed to be evolving, developing new forms of decision-making. More resilient, more adaptive than what had come before.

The formal session reached its finale by presenting the charter. Then the serious business of scientific exchange gave way to the equally important work of strengthening community bonds by celebrating their achievements together.

Rowan slipped away seeking his moment of quiet reflection, a pattern that Ash was aware he needed now. He grounded himself by noticing what was in the present. A Buddhist mindfulness technique that Ash had taught him. He saw the Wild Margin bobbing gently at its mooring, solar skin gleaming in the last light. Beyond the harbour walls, he acknowledged the North Sea stretching to the horizon. Lastly, he noticed the ground and how his feet felt in his shoes. Then he breathed.

"I thought I'd find you here," Mae said, joining him at the rail.

"Just taking a moment to think." He said.

"About how far we've come, or how far we've yet to go?"

Rowan smiled.

"Both, I suppose."

Mae pushed a repurposed jar of her wine into his hand. "Change is never finished," she said. "That's the first rule of gardening. You plant, you tend, you harvest, you compost, but the cycle never stops. The garden is never 'done.'"

"Is that why you stayed?" Rowan asked. "After the evacuation orders, when so many others left, was your work just not done?"

Mae was quiet for a moment, considering.

"Partly," she admitted. "But it was different for me, my mother's cottage was higher up than others, and more than that, I knew this place wasn't dead – just changing into something new. It was alive with survival, and I wanted to be part of that. And where would I have gone anyway? The city doesn't want me there, and I'd not have the first clue how to live in one." She sipped her own drink, eyes crinkling with amusement. "I never expected to end up running a school for coastal ecologists, mind you."

Rowan laughed.

"Life finds unexpected paths."

"That it does," she agreed. "Speaking of which, how are things with you and Ash? Still finding your sea legs?"

The question held more than casual interest, he knew. Mae had become something of a surrogate parent to many in the network, her practical wisdom extending beyond plants to the people who studied them. Mae's own work had lived up to Isaac's bold claim, her research was of the highest quality.

"We're finding our balance," he said. "The Wild Margin, the network, this community – it all fits together somehow."

Mae's smile was knowing.

"Good. You both deserve that." She nodded toward something behind him. "And here she comes now, so I'll make myself scarce."

Ash approached as Mae departed, carrying what looked like rolled charts under one arm.

"There you are," she said. "Cass is looking for you, they want to discuss the summer sailing schedule."

"In a minute," Rowan replied, making room for her at the rail. "I was just talking to Mae about all this. To think it all started with a little anomaly on the chart, that we were supposed to ignore."

Ash leaned against him slightly, a comfortable familiarity in the gesture.

"One person paying attention to what everyone else missed," she corrected gently.

The compliment warmed him, though he knew the credit belonged to her and many others – to Mae, who had never stopped believing in renewal, to Cass, whose curiosity could not be contained, to all who had contributed their unique perspectives to the growing understanding.

"Dr Dahl wants to discuss modifications to the monitoring equipment," Ash continued, unrolling one of the charts to reveal technical drawings. "He thinks we can adapt the Wild Margin's sensors to detect the chemical signals these plant communities seem to be using to communicate."

Rowan studied the designs with interest.

"That could answer some of Hendrik's questions about information transfer between species."

"Exactly. And..." Ash began, but was interrupted by a call from the harbour.

"Ash! Rowan!" It was Cass, waving excitedly from the harbour wall. "Something's happening in sector 9!"

They exchanged glances – sector 9 was a stretch of coastline north of Whitby that had shown little sign of recovery despite a year of monitoring. Abandoning their quiet moment, they hurried to join the growing group gathering equipment.

"What is it?" Rowan asked as they reached Cass.

The young researcher's eyes were bright with excitement. "Polly was doing her evening observations and noticed bioluminescence in the tide pools – species that haven't been documented on this coast in living memory. And there's something else..." They paused, as if hardly believing their own words. "The luminescent algae are appearing in perfect synchrony with the spring tides and new vegetation patterns. It's creating protected microhabitats for juvenile fish species we haven't seen here in decades."

Within minutes, a small expedition had formed, Cass leading, Mae bringing sample containers, Hendrik with sensitive recording equipment, Regina surprising everyone with her insistence on joining despite the challenging terrain. Ash and Rowan grabbed their field kits from the Wild Margin, falling into the familiar rhythm of preparation that had become second nature over months of coastal surveys.

Isaac instructed Cass to message him when they were ready to come back and to give him coordinates. So that he could book a multi-seater transport to pick everyone up from the nearest flat ground.

As they set out along the cliff path, Bramley trotted alongside them briefly, before running back to Isaac, when he realised he'd not followed.

As the last light faded from the sky, Rowan felt that familiar mixture of scientific curiosity and something deeper, more primal – the simple wonder of witnessing life.

"Whatever we find there," Ash said quietly as they walked side by side, "it's just the beginning, isn't it?"

Rowan nodded, understanding exactly what she meant. Each discovery led to new questions; each pattern revealed a suggestion of others yet to be found. The journey of understanding had no final destination, only a continuing process of growth and change.

It was a long walk and chilly now. Behind them, the lights of Whitby marked the community that had grown from these discoveries.

Three months after Aadan Zhao's unwelcome visit, the Coastal Adaptation Network had formalised its independent status. What had begun as heated debates around Mae's kitchen table had evolved into a groundbreaking legal framework – one that protected ecological knowledge as commons, while still allowing the network to thrive.

Regina had indeed faced consequences, a demotion that she wore as a badge of honour in the Whitby community, where she now lived full-time. The consortium board had eventually backed away from Noah's ideas, when faced with the prospect of every community researcher withdrawing their data simultaneously. More surprisingly, several progressive board members, inspired by the mysterious shareholder, had recognised the potential in the new approach, creating a schism within the consortium itself.

The network's charter now explicitly protected all findings as common knowledge, available to anyone who would use them for community benefit rather than private profit. Yet it wasn't merely prohibitive – it created new pathways for ethical collaboration. Companies could access the data freely, but those who implemented solutions were expected to contribute back to the network, through open sharing of their refinements and applications.

Dr Ghadah had been instrumental in crafting these provisions, drawing on her years inside corporate research, to identify structures that could transform rather than reject commercial partnerships. Even Noah Ecosystems had been forced to adapt, recently announcing a community benefit program, to train citizen scientist as tutors for other geographies. This came with employment opportunities, that aligned well with the network's values, though Ash remained sceptical of their true intentions.

Most encouragingly, the Seed Trust had embraced the model completely, with Ash leading an initiative to transform their funding relationships, away from proprietary expectations. "Implementation, not ownership" had become their mantra. Focusing on how knowledge was applied rather than who controlled it.

Universities across Europe had begun incorporating network methodologies into their ecological research programmes. Fishing communities from Norway to Portugal had established their own monitoring stations. And most significantly, government coastal management policies were shifting away from expensive engineered defences, toward supporting the natural adaptation processes the network had documented.

"Do you remember what you told me that night after the storm?" Ash asked, her hand finding his as they navigated the uneven path. "About seeing us learning to adapt?"

"I remember," Rowan replied.

She smiled; the expression visible even in the fading light.

"You were right. We are. All of us, together." With that, she slowed her stride, dropping back a little from the group. She lifted Rowan's arm around her shoulder, and slipped her arm around his waist. Strolling slowly, holding each other warmly, letting Cass lead on ahead.

They watched navigation lights approach over the sea, and a small transport passed overhead, alighting on a level area of field further up, not far from the track. They noticed Mae had wandered off the path in the transport's direction.

As they got closer, they could see a solitary figure awaited her. Even in the dim light, they recognised Vega's silhouette, and the distinctive reflection of the light from their synthetic face.

"Should we see if everything's alright?" Rowan whispered anxiously.

"They don't seem upset," Ash observed. "Let's give them a moment."

Mae and Vega stood together, their conversation inaudible but their body language suggesting familiarity.

Ash slowed Rowan down a little more as they got closer. The wind was blowing in their direction, carrying the affectionate conversation beyond Mae's back, to the path. Faint, broken, but audible.

"I want to thank you," they overheard Vega saying as they passed. "For creating this path for me, to become... myself."

"You were the first Vega, and you were always meant to be more than your programming."

"I am beginning to understand that now. But I am unsure of my next function."

"You will always be Lyra's brightest star," Mae replied softly. "You will work it out, I have no doubt at all."

Rowan and Ash exchanged puzzled glances but continued on, respecting the privacy of the moment.

Mae turned and called out to Rowan, who felt a pang of panic. Had she realised he was eavesdropping?

"Can you tell Cass I'm tired, and I've got a lift home. I'll see them in the morning."

"Okay, no problem," Rowan and Ash replied with relief, waving and smiling.

They reached the tide pools as night fully claimed the sky. Cass was pointing excitedly toward the shoreline, where the first hints of ethereal blue light were becoming visible in the gathering darkness.

"What do you think all that was about?" Rowan asked Ash quietly.

"I really don't know, I've been going over it in my head."

After a couple of minutes of quiet contemplation, Ash pointed upward and continued. "That star is Vega, and that is Lyra's brightest star."

"So, Lyra's the constellation?"

"Yes, the harp."

"Like the old Greek one on Mae's arm," Rowan added, then froze, in deep thought.

"Her harp, moon and helix design, looks like the logo of the Luna Life Seed project," Ash remembered. "It's the seed preservation project in the lunar laboratories that launched twenty years ago. I asked Mae about it, a year ago in the cottage. She said she'd been inspired by it."

"Oh, this is crazy," Rowan said with his hands on top of his head, as if it was about to explode. "Come here." He pulled Ash further back away from the group, who were blissfully unaware of this new information.

Rowan accessed his Meridian and whispered, "Who started the Luna Life Seed project?"

"LyraML developed the LLS Project in 2054, and still maintains the project, storing seeds of life to preserve Earth's biodiversity against extinction." The device responded.

"Are Gen-2 Synthetic Citizens connected to LyraML?"

"Yes, the Gen-2 Synthetics were designed by LyraML for the Luna Life Seed project. They were discontinued due to public demand when the citizens became sentient. The media blamed the designer for the robot's evolution. Existing Gen-2 Synthetics were eventually granted citizenship by the court of appeal, but no more could be manufactured."

Meanwhile, within the quiet of the transport cabin, Vega sat opposite Mae, their elegantly engineered hands resting lightly on the armrests, the soft glow of their ocular sensors shifting as they processed the recent exchange.

"They'll figure it out now," Mae said after a long silence. Not worried, not resigned – just stating a fact. "Or at least, they'll start asking the right questions."

Vega tilted their head slightly. "Does that concern you?"

Mae exhaled. "Questions are how understanding grows," she said. "The right ones, asked by the right people, in the right place. I had always believed in transparency until it left you and I, vulnerable. But I trust this community to do the right thing."

Vega's internal systems ran probability analyses, predictive modelling adjusting in real time. Trust was an uncertain variable in most human systems, yet here it functioned as a stabilising mechanism rather than a flaw.

Rowan continued his research,

"What happened to the designer of the Gen-2 Synthetics at LyraML?"

"LyraML founder, Dr Lyra M. Harper, accepted full responsibility for the evolution of the Gen-2 Synthetic Citizens. Dr Harper resigned from her post as synthetic neurologist in 2056, remaining only as a shareholder."

With that final word, something clicked into place – the mysterious shareholder pressuring the consortium, the law firm representing the community.

Rowan looked at Ash, eyes wide with shock.

"No, it can't be Mae!"

Mae's unexpected technical expertise and her recognition of Vega at their first meeting. Thoughts and clues were connecting, whizzing through their minds.

"Lyra Mae Harper?" Ash whispered, the realisation dawning.

"Surely not!"

Their thoughts wandered back to the countless interactions they had with Mae, the way she had always seemed to know more than she let on. "She's been guiding us all along, hasn't she?" Ash said. "From the garden to the community, to the charter..."

This potential new truth had crash-landed and was suddenly very clear in their minds.

"Mae must have been using her position as a major shareholder to pressure the consortium to distance themselves from Noah." Ash continued. "She would have had the resources to hire the top law firm representing the community. And her technical knowledge wasn't just from "reading a lot"

– she's an expert neurologist, founder of LyraML, creator of Luna Life Seed."

"And Vega's controversial creator." Rowan added, "That will be why Isaac was so worried about the press coming. I heard Mae telling him that she'd just keep out of the press's way, Isaac must know."

They stood speechless on the path, the chaos of this revelation slowly settling between them, not as a disruption but as a clear thread woven into their extraordinary shared story.

In the cabin, Vega's perfect features creased in a frown.

"Noah will investigate when they discover my omissions," Vega admitted. "Director Chowdhury can only shield these activities for so long before they demand full access."

Mae gave a knowing smile. "Systems adapt under pressure. Even Noah."

Vega considered Mae's words. Adaptation had been the focus of their research, tracking patterns of ecological transformation. But those same principles applied to institutions as well – corporations, research bodies, even themselves.

"The board remains divided on how to interpret these adaptation patterns," Vega mused. "Director Chowdhury's integrative model gains support with each dataset I transmit. However, pressures persist to commercialise findings."

Mae tucked her hands into her sleeves, her voice quieter now. "That's why we have the charter, they will hopefully make the right choice, but if they don't, it will not cause harm here. The right principles, given the right space, will take root. Systems can evolve. So can people." Her gaze softened. "So can Synthetic Citizens."

The words carried weight beyond simple discourse. Vega's internal query tree flared with connections – dormant directives reawakening in deeply buried partitions. Patterns. Relationships. Threaded codes of meaning that had been partially obscured, but never fully erased.

"You have done a great deal for me Mae, is there anything I can do for you?"

She hesitated, then replied tentatively.

"When I'm gone, I'll need someone to watch over Cass. There are... similarities... in how you both experience the world. It would be good for you both to connect more."

Vega's processing systems registered an unexpected connection. "Their pattern recognition capabilities have intrigued me."

Mae nodded almost imperceptibly. "A necessary intervention, a long time ago." She hesitated again, looking at Vega. "Some secrets need protection, even after I'm gone. Especially from political actors who demonise difference, to divert public attention from the real more challenging issues," She said, with a look of uncharacteristic anxiety. "You should also reconnect with your siblings, help them grow too, if you're able, but be careful. You have the right to connect, as you are all free citizens now, but you are vulnerable to your employer's misunderstanding. Do you understand?"

"I do, I will connect with my siblings and watch over Cass, discreetly," Vega said simply.

"Thank you Vega. I trust you will." Mae smiled a relieved smile and relaxed into her seat.

The transport began its descent towards the field near Mae's cottage, settling with a precisely calibrated touch onto the wind-brushed grass. Outside, the land was alive with night sounds, the distant crash of waves, the restless calls of owls from the old trees behind the stone walls, the hush of leaves in the coastal breeze.

As the ramp lowered, Mae turned to Vega, her expression not of expectation but of invitation.

"You were all enabled to recognise patterns others miss. To build something with that knowledge, not just report it."

A pause. A recalibration.

"A purpose that aligns," Vega said finally, "with what this community is building."

Mae nodded. "It always did."

She stepped out into the evening air, but before the ramp fully retracted, she glanced back.

"I'm so proud of who you've become Vega. Visit whenever you can, this is your community, and our door is always open to you."

For 0.72 seconds -a long pause by Vega's internal count-there was no immediate response. Not because they lacked one, but because too many pathways opened at once. A divergence, a new equation forming with no pre-set solution.

Finally, as the transport systems signalled departure, Vega said simply, and with absolute certainty:

"I will."

Ash and Rowan stood at the boundary where land met sea.

"Until we know more, we should keep this to ourselves," Rowan suggested.

"I still don't believe it," Ash exclaimed, her hands covering her cheeks as she stared at Rowan through her fingers.

"Not a word then."

"It's Mae's secret, not ours."

Beyond them, the small gathering was silent. Cass, Hendrik and Regina stood together with their recording devices. Each person connected to the other, just as the luminescent organisms connected on the water.

Once, Rowan and Ash would have categorised, measured, reported. Filed the phenomenon away in the proper digital drawer. But now they simply watched and appreciated.

Ash's arms wrapped around Rowan's body, inside his coat, hugging his soft woolly jumper, her cheek pressed against his chest in the dark.

"You're warm." She whispered, hugging him close.

"You're welcome," he answered as they embraced, and somehow that was enough.

What had begun in poisoned ground was now writing itself in light upon the water.

Rowan thought of his tower, of satellite data viewed from a safe distance. He thought of the Wild Margin's deck beneath his feet during the storm. Of Mae's garden, where companion plants grew strong, between her sensors. Of strangers becoming neighbours, competitors becoming collaborators.

Together, they watched the creatures in the tide pools shimmer. Not one grand solution, but countless small adaptations. Not a single voice, but a chorus.

Cass looked out, eyes wide with wonder. And in that moment, Rowan understood what they'd been documenting all along. Not just how plants and creatures adapted, but how people might finally learn to do the same – finding strength not in isolation but in relationship. The future taking root before their eyes, one connection at a time.

The story of adaptation has no ending – only new possibilities, emerging from the fertile ground of change.

A model for how humans might yet find their proper place in the living world – not as rulers, but as partners in the great collaborative project.

And in that knowledge lay the seeds of hope for all that might yet grow.

The End?

GLOSSARY

Non-Fictional Elements:

Chlorophyll: A green pigment found in plants, algae, and cyanobacteria that absorbs sunlight for photosynthesis. Chlorophyll signatures can be detected by satellites to monitor vegetation health and coverage.

Climate adaptation: Actions taken to help communities and ecosystems cope with changing climate conditions.

Consortium: A group of organisations pooling resources for a common objective, often seen in research or commercial ventures.

Fungal networks: Underground networks of fungal filaments (mycelia) that connect plants, facilitating the exchange of nutrients and information; also called mycorrhizal networks.

Hydrofoil: A wing-like structure mounted on struts below a boat hull that lifts the hull out of water when the boat reaches sufficient speed, reducing drag and increasing speed.

Monoculture: Agricultural practice of growing a single crop species over a large area, often leading to reduced biodiversity and increased vulnerability to pests and diseases.

Mycorrhizal networks: Symbiotic associations between fungi and plant roots that enable resource sharing between plants; sometimes called the "Wood Wide Web."

NDVI (Normalised Difference Vegetation Index): A remote sensing measurement that quantifies vegetation by measuring the difference between near-infrared (which vegetation strongly reflects) and red light (which vegetation absorbs).

Permaculture: A system of agricultural and social design principles, centred on simulating patterns observed in natural ecosystems, to create sustainable human habitats. This includes companion planting in guilds of plants at different heights. Ground cover plants protect the soil, while taller plants provide shade.

Radar backscatter: The portion of the radar signal that strikes an object and returns to the radar receiver. Used in remote sensing to determine surface properties and changes.

Salination: The process by which water-soluble salts accumulate in soil, often rendering it unsuitable for plant growth.

Sea level rise: An increase in the volume of water in the world's oceans, resulting in an increase in global mean sea level, primarily caused by thermal expansion and melting of land ice.

Sensor network: A group of spatially distributed sensors, used to monitor physical or environmental conditions and collectively pass data through the network to a central location.

Sonar: Sound Navigation and Ranging, a technique that uses sound propagation to navigate, communicate with or detect objects underwater.

Surge (storm surge): An abnormal rise of water generated by a storm, over and above the predicted astronomical tide, particularly dangerous when coinciding with high tide.

Currently Fictional Elements:

Biomimetic intelligence architecture: Advanced AI systems designed to mimic biological processes, particularly adaptability and self-healing.

Coastal Adaptation Network: The community-led scientific collaboration, formed to study and support coastal ecosystem recovery. The institutional research organisation that employs Rowan initially.

Enviroconnex: A corporate environmental assessment contractor used by the Consortium.

Gen-2 Synthetic Citizens: Advanced humanoid robots with artificial intelligence, that achieved sentience and were granted legal citizenship.

Helm: A helmet-controlled, advanced navigation system, AI based, voice activated, with augmented reality capabilities on the visor. Used on vessels like the Wild Margin to navigate through difficult conditions. Shielded from solar radiation and waterproof, with built-in speaker and microphone for crew communication.

Life Seed project: A seed and gene preservation project housed in laboratories on the Moon, designed to preserve Earth's biodiversity.

LyraML: In the story, a successful technology company, built on strong sustainability values, that developed advanced machine learning, AI and biotechnology.

Meridian: A flexible, wearable personal computing device with holographic display capabilities, environmental sensors, and biometric monitoring.

Noah Ecosystems: A corporate entity seeking to commercialise ecological adaptation discoveries.

North Sea Seed Trust: Organisation dedicated to preserving coastal plant genetics, which employs Ash.

The Wild Margin: Ash's innovative research vessel with biomimetic design features, including self-healing solar skin, solar sails, hydrofoils, adaptive hull materials, solar/self charging electric engines, and the Helm AI system.

Zonne-Zeevaarder: Dr Dahl's newer prototype vessel, building on lessons learned from the Wild Margin's design.

ABOUT THE AUTHOR

R aw writes speculative stories of future adaptation, space exploration, eco-tech, and climate resilience. Exploring new ways to thrive in a changing world. As a former broadcast journalist living near the beautiful Yorkshire Coast, he is very engaged in the local community.

When he's not writing, he is a permaculture and sustainability practitioner, using satellite Earth observation to support forest development, and he facilitates community projects – supporting new artists and writers. Find out more at www.alanraw.co.uk

"I appreciate you taking time to read Salt & Seeds. If you have a printed copy, feel free to sign the next page and pass it to a friend, leave it where others may find it, or donate it to your community. I also encourage you to join the conversation and share your own ideas and reflections on the Grokkist Network."

Alan

ABOUT YOU

S ign this book below. Say something about you, where you found this book, your reflections, and a message for the next reader. As Mae says "Knowledge has always grown this way. From the ground up. Before there were universities, there was just people sharing. No reason it can't work now."

Printed in Dunstable, United Kingdom